Jane W. Gemmill

Notes on Washington

Six years at the national capital

Jane W. Gemmill

Notes on Washington
Six years at the national capital

ISBN/EAN: 9783337230838

Printed in Europe, USA, Canada, Australia, Japan

Cover: Foto ©Andreas Hilbeck / pixelio.de

More available books at **www.hansebooks.com**

NOTES ON WASHINGTON,

OR

SIX YEARS AT THE NATIONAL CAPITAL.

BY

JANE W. GEMMILL.

PHILADELPHIA:
E. CLAXTON & COMPANY.
930 MARKET STREET.
1884.

COLLINS, PRINTER.

PREFACE.

I HAVE not attempted to write a history of Washington in the following pages, nor to closely follow the march of events. My attention has been more particularly directed toward places and subjects of general interest, and likely to prove entertaining to those who, by reason of residing at a great distance, or from want of opportunity, are unable to visit the Capital. Of the events that occurred during my sojourn of six years, I have noted only the most remarkable. Some of these Notes were originally published in the *National Republican*, of Washington City.

J. W. G.

September 4, 1883.

CONTENTS.

NOTES ON WASHINGTON.

———◆———

I.

THE CITY.

IT was John Randolph, I believe, who said that
Washington is "a city of magnificent distances,"
to which he might add, were he living now, magnificent residences and magnificent public buildings.

Everything is upon a grand scale. The broad
avenues are broader than those of any other city I
have seen. Acres and acres of highly cultivated
land are inclosed in parks and public grounds.
Whole squares are taken up by imposing piles of
granite and marble. Beautiful vistas open in every
direction—terminating here with a handsome work
of art, there with a stately building, or finally lost
to view in the mist and hills beyond the city.

The location is remarkably attractive. On the
south is the broad Potomac River; on the east the
Anacostia, or Eastern Branch; and on the north and

2

west a circle of beautifully wooded hills. The surface is very undulating, but the elevations and depressions so gradual one scarcely realizes how much the altitude varies at different points.

The city abounds with places of interest to the sojourner or tourist, and one may while away days and even weeks and not begin to exhaust their treasures. And then, too, all these places are free! Lovers of art have free access three days in the week to galleries of painting and statuary. Extensive museums stored with relics, minerals and curiosities are open to all who care to enter. The Congressional Library is open every day in the week (with the exception of public holidays) to the student or reader; who can sit in quiet nooks and enjoy the rich feast spread before him.

Public business is conducted upon a grand scale, and the several departments, with their miles of tessellated corridors, busy clerks and rush of important business, afford quite as much entertainment as the places specially designed for the purpose.

The Capitol, the old houses, the churches, cemeteries and environs each have an interest of their own, and the incidents and legends forming a part of their history are well worth hearing.

II.

CAPITOL.

HOW very interesting the Capitol is! And yet one can scarcely define what this great interest consists in. It is not in the marble walls, Corinthian columns and graceful dome. Not in the works of art—for the collection is meagre, and, with some few exceptions, decidedly commonplace. Not in the elaborate gilding, tasteful frescoes and choice mosaics; for in these things many private residences in the country far surpass it. Not in the vast proportions of the rotunda, nor in the mysterious recesses of the crypt. I think it is more in the sentiment than the reality. The historical associations no doubt lend an interest; then, too, the national pride is gratified in finding such a stately building for the meetings of Congress—the great Sun around which the whole political system revolves, the engine as it were which starts and moves every part of

the Governmental machinery. There is also a sense
of ownership. It is our Capitol; we helped to rear
it, or if we did not our fathers and grandfathers did,
and therefore ours by right of inheritance.

How extremely interesting it is to sit in the galleries and look down upon the two houses of Congress in session! How pleasant to listen to the
debates and to become personally acquainted with
the men whose names have been so familiar to us
through the public press! To see our hero of many
political battles hold the Senate or House in close
attention by his eloquence, and to find instead of
being disenchanted, our admiration for him increased
threefold!

There is great pleasure always in walking about
the old Hall of Representatives, and in imagination
going over the past and recalling the exciting scenes
enacted there during the years immediately preceding the late war.

It is so very contracted in space, we cannot cease
to wonder where the audience was seated, which
crowded in during that memorable two months
balloting for Speaker in 1856. It is a handsome
apartment, and quite appropriate for the purpose to
which at present applied, viz., Statuary Hall. The

statues of a number of distinguished men are collected there; among them Green, Williams, Clinton, Trumbull, Sherman, Winthrop, Adams, Allen, Jefferson, Hamilton, and Lincoln; also the mosaic portrait of Lincoln—the gift of an Italian city to the United States—and a beautiful allegorical clock. The design of this clock is unique. The figure of History is standing in a winged car or chariot, which represents Time passing over the globe, and in her hand a scroll upon which she inscribes passing events. The wheel of the car forms the dial-plate of the clock. The whole is cut from fine Carrara marble and cost $2000.

The hall is Grecian in design, with a dome supported by twenty-two columns of variegated marble. These are highly polished and finished with capitals of Carrara marble. The floor is inlaid with blocks of black and white marble.

One enters the Supreme Court room with a feeling of awe—not inspired though by the presence of the august body belonging there—but by the knowledge it was in this hall Webster, Clay, Calhoun, Clayton and the other great men contemporary with them, directed national affairs and exhibited that wonderful brilliancy of intellect which so justly entitled them to be ranked as stars of the first magnitude in the political firmament.

So much has happened in the history of our country since their time, it seems as though they must have lived and died ages ago; and yet I am constantly meeting with persons who enjoyed the privilege of hearing them speak in this room, and of witnessing many scenes that have become historical, and they are not very old persons either. They always become enthusiastic when speaking of Mr. Webster's eloquence, and of his appearance upon the floor. How he would throw his shoulders back, expand his chest and roll out his mighty sentences, his black eyes gleaming all the while like great coals of fire.

They all without exception dwell upon the point of Mr. Webster being a plain speaker, and how greatly surprised those persons were—who expected him to indulge in high-sounding rhetorical phrases, and beautiful imagery far above the ordinary comprehension—when they heard him speak.

It is related of a countryman then living in Virginia, who having heard of the great orator at Washington, determined the next time business called him to the city, to go to the Capitol to hear him.

The opportunity soon offered and he took his seat in the gallery. He had not been there very long when a Senator arose and commenced speaking.

The stranger, who did not know Mr. Webster by sight, became very much interested in what he was saying, so much so, that he turned to his neighbor and asked the name of the speaker. "Webster," was the answer. "Ah, no," returned the stranger, "it cannot be Webster, for that man has not said a blamed word yet I could not easily understand!"

"Comparisons are odious," I very well know, and one never gets any thanks for drawing them; but, evidently the leaders of that period must have been greatly over-rated and those of the present time under-rated; or, the Senate of thirty years ago was a far more able body than that of to-day.

It may not be admitted by all, but nowadays brains, learning, and legal experience do not seem to be of half as much importance in making a man eligible for a seat as gold. The gold-weighted member is usually harmless, and rarely becomes a leader, yet he makes his presence felt, and by his presence disbars another from entering who in time might become a bright and shining light.

The Capitol as it stands to-day is a grand monu-

ment to republican progress and liberality. Every
one knows there are defects, and many of them quite
prominent, but these are not due to any stint in the
expenditures, nor to defects in the original plan of
the founders. They are due rather to a determination upon the part of Congress in the past, to employ foreign artists, many of whom were of doubtful
skill, and also to the peculiar ideas of individuals
regarding the fitness of things. As is well known,
many works of art have been accepted and a large
price paid for them, not on account of their intrinsic
merit, but because the artist was fortunate enough to
have a friend upon the purchasing committee, and
by numerous interviews, some judicious flattery, and
maybe a terrapin supper, managed to make them all
believe that the particular painting or statue awaiting their decision was quite as artistic as one could
hope for since the loss of the *old masters!*

When one remembers that the Capitol covers
three and one-half acres of ground, and that the
interior is a perfect labyrinth of passages, rooms,
and recesses, he can readily understand how much
time and money might be expended upon it without
making very much show, and also how utterly impossible to give a description that would be at all

satisfactory. The compilers of the guide-books have handled the subject with great skill; but one must enter the building, spend days and weeks in examining the details to form a correct idea of its vastness, beauty, and great cost. About the cost much might be said, and much speculation indulged in; probably the exact figures cannot be ascertained, but it is safe to say from $15,000,000 to $25,000,000 have been already expended.

The dome is the crowning beauty of the whole pile—without it the building would be flat, insipid, and characterless. It can be seen from all parts of the city and several distant points in the surrounding country: the effect of the setting sun upon it, when viewed from these distant points, is sometimes very beautiful. The bronze Goddess of Liberty appears as though made of burnished gold, and the rays of sunlight reflected from the innumerable windows around the upper part, give it the appearance of being brilliantly illuminated with crimson lights. Although it is constructed of iron and weighs over 8,000,000 pounds, it seems to rest like a snowy bubble in mid air; and its proportions are so graceful, its color so attractive, one never wearies of it, nor does it become monotonous and commonplace.

Entering the rotunda from the east side, the visitor passes through the great Bronze Door, modelled by Rogers in Rome in 1858, and cast in Munich by Von Miller in 1860. This door stands nineteen feet high and cost $28,000. The embellishments consist of the principal events in the life of Columbus and the discovery of America, and are interesting and beautiful.

The smaller bronze door in the main entrance to the Senate wing was cast in this country. It is also very beautifully embellished in alto relievo with historical events connected with the establishment of our Independence. These doors are very elegant, but much of their beauty is obscured by a thick coating of dust. Washington being an exceedingly dusty city, the tiny particles enter every crevice, and constant watchfulness is necessary to keep the statues, relievos, and other works of art in the Capitol free from them. This duty, however, is not attended to as it should be, and I think it would be a good thing in Congress to appropriate a certain sum each year for the salaries of a corps of sweepers and dusters, whose duty should be to dust off at least once a week, the "Head of Columbus," the feet and ruff of Winthrop, the heavy cloak of " Brother Jonathan," and the statues of other distinguished persons near. I am sure the pleasure of sight-seers would be greatly increased thereby. A few thousand dollars less each year for contested election cases would furnish the requisite sum.

Some of the most elaborately decorated parts of the Capitol are rarely seen by the public, and so badly lighted that when seen, the beauty of the work cannot be discerned. This is particularly true of the passage and bronze staircase leading to the lobby of the Senate. The hallway is richly frescoed in birds, foliage, and animals, and much time and labor expended upon the work. On account of being below the main floor, strangers seldom go there, and it is used only by employés and persons intent upon business. The latter are usually too much absorbed or too hurried to note the beauty of the delicate ferns, grasses, and clinging tendrils; or too indifferent to inquire whether the brilliant bird poised so gracefully before them is a robin or a pigeon, or whether it hails from the tropics or their neighbor's barnyard. And the bronze staircase is so dark one cannot see the beautiful embellishments, consisting of vines and boughs, laughing Cupids, serpents, and spread eagles.

The President's Room in the Senate wing is very tastefully decorated. The work was done by Brumidi, the Italian artist who spent nearly a lifetime in working upon the Capitol. There are large medallions containing portraits of Washington, Franklin, Jefferson, and other illustrious men; beautiful scroll work and numerous allegorical figures. A superb chandelier depends from the ceiling, and the room is luxuriously furnished. The President uses the room the last day or days of a session of Congress, when it is necessary to expedite business; and remains there with his Cabinet to pass upon and sign such bills as meet his approval.

Another beautiful room is the marble room, used by the Senators for receiving their friends. The walls are of Tennessee marble, having large mirrors inserted, forming panels. The floor is inlaid with colored tiles and the roof supported by a double row of fluted columns. The mirrors reflect these columns and the effect is quite fine.

When Congress is in session the average visitor gives very little attention to the beauties of the Capitol. He is usually too much absorbed and interested in the deliberations going on in the Senate and House to spare much time for an examination of pictures, marbles, and frescoes; and very many pass them by without bestowing so much as a thought or glance upon them.

The House of Representatives usually claims the largest share of attention, and is always more popular than the Senate; I have observed that at least two out of every three find their way to the galleries of the former. The first visit is always unsatisfactory. There is such confusion, such noise, so many walking about, so much apparent indifference upon the part of members, such a tangle of rules and resolutions, and points of order, such a lack of dignity, the visitor becomes dazed and impatient, and frequently disgusted. But after many visits he becomes accustomed to the confusion; he learns to locate prominent members, and catches a glimpse here and there of the thread of business; he reads the daily report of the proceedings, and finally becomes deeply interested. It then becomes more fascinating than any place of amusement; better than the theatre, for the acting at the theatre is only acting after all, while here, real life; better than the circus, for instead of one or two clowns to furnish amusement for the audience there are frequently a dozen and more. And there is also a pleasurable anticipation before one, never furnished by places of amusement—the carefully prepared programme of the latter always showing precisely what one is to expect; but in the House of Representatives you do not know at what moment a storm of excitement may burst upon you, which almost lifts you from your seat, or what mine may be sprung by an imperceptible spark to bring confusion and dismay upon the floor. Very true, one is obliged to take the bitter with the sweet, for all the speakers are not eloquent, nor all learned and cultivated.

Then, too, if you are a lover of history, you enjoy looking down upon the scene, and the men whose names and legislative acts will help to fill the pages of future American history; and you also find keen pleasure in noting how strangely history repeats itself in each succeeding generation. Sitting in the gallery of the House one day, just after reading a chapter in Macaulay's History of England, describing the scenes and debates in the British House of Commons of two hundred years ago, I found myself mentally substituting House of Representatives for "House of Commons," Republican and Democrat for "Whig and Tory," appropriation bill for "bill of supply," and surprised to find how nicely the description suited the scene before me.

Our Congress though has learned some things to perfection, which Parliament had not learned two hundred years ago.

Macaulay says: "It does not appear, however, that the parliamentary tacticians of the seventeenth century were aware of the extent to which a small number of members can, without violating any form, retard the course of business." Filibustering has been reduced to a science at our Capitol, and it has come to be an acknowledged fact, that the skilful management of the minority by a capable leader can accomplish quite as much as a badly managed majority.

Going from the House of Representatives to the Senate, is like going from the torrid to the frigid zone, or like going from an uproarious mass-meeting to a Friends' meeting, waiting for the Spirit to move them. The contrast is so great. Some persons enjoy the change, and experience a sense of relief upon taking their seat in the gallery of the latter, while others are so chilled and depressed by the quiet dignity pervading the chamber, they find little pleasure in remaining.

Upon rare occasions I have seen considerable excitement manifested in the Senate and applause from the galleries break out repeatedly, in spite of threats from the presiding officer to have them cleared if it were persisted in.

Three hundred and seventy-one steps to the Dome; but who cares for steps when such a glorious, beautiful view is opened before him? Who thinks of fatigue, when by climbing so high he can with a glance take in the whole District of Columbia, parts of the States of Maryland and Virginia, and with the eye follow the winding Potomac many miles on its journey to the sea?

Looking west, the city—with its spires and parks, dancing fountains, wide avenues and handsome public buildings—is spread out before you like a beautiful picture. Away off in the distance the heights of Georgetown, enveloped in haze, form a charming background to the picture and keep silent watch over the old town nestled in the valley below. Turning to the north the Howard University is a prominent and pleasing feature of the landscape, and away beyond it the tower and flag of the Soldiers' Home can be plainly seen. Like a black line stretching across the country is the track of the Baltimore and Ohio Railroad, and the eye can follow its course for many miles.

During the war this great thoroughfare was the artery which supplied the life-blood to the Capital, and through it to the nation. How jealously it was guarded during those trying times! And though the duty was considered dull and monotonous, by those desiring an opportunity to win glory in the field, it was of equal importance in view of the final result.

If they had the power of speech those iron rails might whisper strange stories of the countless multitude passing over them. They might tell us of ambitious statesmen journeying to the Capital dreaming of future greatness; of scheming politicians intent upon gaining their selfish ends; of Presidents on their way to take oath of office and receive the confirmation of the love and confidence of a happy, intelligent people; of fair women returning again and again to the fashionable circle where they have reigned with so much grace; of faithful friends with hearts filled with sadness, bearing away the inanimate form of some dear one to its last rest-

ing place, and more than all of that wonderful transportation of men and munitions of war, which never
ceased day nor night while the rebellion lasted.

This road was deeply in debt at the beginning of
the war, but by the time it had distributed the last
regiment of soldiers to their homes had a large sur-
plus on the credit side.

Looking out over the circle of hills surrounding
the city, it is hard to realize that not quite a score
of years ago they were crowned with fortifications,
and the plains below white with the tents of an encamped army.   To-day the hills are beautiful with
trees and shrubbery decked in their most bewitching
spring attire, and the slopes are covered with luxuriant pastures in which the lazy cattle brouse unmo-
lested.   Instead of flashing bayonets, the rippling
waters of the Potomac catch the sunbeams, and with
a thrill of pleasure we realize "all is quiet along the
Potomac;" but a different quiet from that wont to
fly over the wires, sending comfort for the time to
thousands of anxious homes North and South.   It
is the quiet of peace, and the historic old river flows
on, forgetting the part it took in that struggle; flows
on past the city of the dead on Arlington Heights;

past the ancient town of Alexandria with its grass-grown streets; past the home and tomb of Washington; past happy homesteads, where infant sons and daughters are being trained to take the places of the fathers and mothers of the present, and, as it flows, softly whispers, "Peace!"

III.

March 1, 1877.

"THE Electoral Commission" is a new term in American politics. A remarkable interest has been excited in its deliberations, and I think far exceeds that taken in public affairs during the troubled period of sectional animosity preceding the late war.

The time for completing its work is being rapidly shortened, and the eyes of the fifty millions of people are turned toward the Capital anxiously awaiting the result. The city is filled with strangers, and a great crowd has surged around the doors and thronged the corridors of the Capitol for several days, making it necessary to issue tickets of admission to the galleries of the Senate and House of Representatives.

I was fortunate this morning in securing a ticket for the latter, and still more fortunate in securing an eligible seat in the front row of benches on the Democratic side of the hall.

It was an impressive scene when the House came to order, and one long to be remembered. Every seat was taken upon the floor and in the galleries, and every inch of standing room occupied.

The morning sunbeams, scattered and softened by the richly stained glass of the skylight, filled the hall with a subdued mellow light. The vivid colors of the National ensign draped back of the Speaker's chair; the rich gilding of the cornices and panels, and the white robes of the Chaplain, were all in keeping with the dramatic aspect of the scene.

Every grade of society was represented in the vast assembly. Learned judges sat shoulder to shoulder with plain citizens; uniformed officers and distinguished legislators stood side by side with humble laborers; and mothers, wives, and fair daughters availed themselves of every proffered seat.

Nothing extraordinary, however, occurred until the two houses met in joint convention, and at one stage of the proceedings, the Senate withdrew to its chamber to debate upon the objections to the decision of the Commission regarding the vote of one of the contested States. The debate then became very warm and acrimonious; and the filibusters wildly renewed their efforts to prevent the completion of the count.

The Speaker, with pale brow and compressed lips, endeavored to maintain control of the House. He pounded the gavel vigorously and called refractory members to order, but the tactics of the filibusters made order almost impossible. The time is now so short they feel each hour lessens their opportunity, and consequently grow more bold and defiant. I can never forget the sensations I experienced when Representative Beebe, of New York, so far forgot himself in the excitement and his efforts to obtain recognition, as to leap from desk to desk, his hand stretched above his head, clasping a sheet of paper which he frantically waved, shouting, Mr. Speaker! Mr. Speaker!

The effect upon the House was something indescribable and the uproar for a few minutes very great. The cold chills crept over me, and I noticed the ladies seated near me turn pale with excitement.

The confusion was soon quelled. The Sergeant-at-Arms walked down the aisle with his mace, which had a magical effect, and in a very short time the House proceeded with the business of the day.

IV.

DEPARTMENTAL LIFE.

DOES anybody outside of Washington have an idea of what life is in a Government Department? It is entirely different from any other calling. First, there is the scramble for appointment, the weary waiting and hope deferred day after day; the rushing around after influential friends to urge the claim of the applicant for the place desired; innumerable visits and letters to the head of the Department; and finally the assignment to duty.

All this precedes entrance upon official life, whether in the capacity of copyist, first, second, or third class clerk.

Then follow the long weary days sitting at a desk trying to do something one has never tried before. Becoming an object to be stared at and whispered about by the other clerks, who are always curious to know what kind of hand he or she writes, what

State they hail from, and upon what roll they are paid.

The days, weeks, and months pass and the new-comer, if at all bright and capable, begins to understand the work before him and to feel pretty well acquainted with his fellow clerks; and here comes the most trying part of official life. No one, except those who have been employed, knows what it is to be shut up in a room with the same people seven hours, six days every week; people from as many different parts of the country as there are individuals, and with quite as many different opinions. No two with the same religious belief. Some highly cultured and some without any culture at all. The majority so puffed up with their own importance as to imagine great danger to the wheels of Government and probably stoppage, if by chance they should die, resign, or be dismissed.

Conversation never flags for want of a subject, and it is enough to turn one's brain to hear the various topics introduced and discussed in the course of the day, and the different hobbies ventilated. Almost every man has a hobby, whatever his position in life, but it really seems as if those of the Government clerk have no equal outside.

The financial schemes introduced from time to time are wonderful. It is the sleeping and waking dream of the average clerk to become rich, or at least independent enough to resign; and yet he never for one moment imagines this to be attained by self-denial, economy, or small savings. Oh no! Some lucky investment in a lottery ticket is to draw a coveted prize, or a good speculation may surprise him, or a rise in mining stocks suddenly make him a millionaire.

It is very remarkable how the ideas of the clerk change and enlarge after a few years' residence in Washington. Away off in his country home a good suit was made to do service for more than one season, and an interesting book or agreeable companion afforded sufficient entertainment for his evenings. But after a sojourn there in Government employ he must have a new suit for every change of season; a new neck-tie to match each suit, and gloves to match the neck-tie; a cane to match the gloves, a scarf-pin to match the cane, and a hat to match all. Every evening there must be tickets to the theatre or opera, or a carriage to the ball, or a dainty little supper at some fashionable café.

If a lady clerk—but the pen must move gently

dealing with them, for a large number of the female clerks are noble, self-sacrificing women, forced to enter upon this life through loss of father, husband, or the demands of dependent little ones, and the ouside world has no knowledge of the struggles they make, or what privations they endure in providing for those loved ones. There are in every office, though, some ladies who do not have burdens to bear, and of them it has been observed, how entirely the womanly weakness for personal adornment takes possession. In what dainty costumes they always appear, and how they love to display pretty little pieces of jewelry and becoming laces!

Although the life is a plodding one, and far more reality than romance about it, the latter is not altogether absent; for more than one Romeo has there found his Juliet. Youthful couples thrown so constantly together frequently become interested in each other, and before they are aware the dangerous little god has marked them for his own. The other clerks enjoy watching the progress of the *affaire du cœur*, while the love-stricken parties innocently imagine it is known only to themselves. After a time—probably some day at the close of business—the lady bids adieu to those around her, and quietly remarks she is not coming back any more.

The clerks in the several Departments are far from being ignorant, as a class, although some may be entitled to the charge. There are poets, historians, philosophers, and theologians among them of no mean attainments. Various causes have led them to the city and to these positions. They have drifted thither upon the wave of circumstances from all parts of the country; from the bleak, rugged hills of New England, and the sunny region of the orange and palmetto; from the mountains and vales of the Western Territories and the golden fields of California. Many boast of an ancestry distinguished in this country and the old world. Many at one time possessed both wealth and influence. If the story of some—for many have a history—could be written out it would be more thrilling and interesting than the most sensational modern novel.

The life is a very good one for discipline, and two or three years of such employment—but not any longer, for after that time a clerk is apt to settle down in a rut and remain there—two or three years of such discipline helps to form character and gives a man better command of himself.

V.

NEGROES.

THE leap from slavery to citizenship made by
the negroes of America was an extraordinary
one, and their deportment under the changed condition highly commendable. In Northern towns and
cities where they are found in small numbers, they
have almost lost their identity as a distinct race, for
their ways of living, acting, and general characteristics are so much like their white brethren, they ex-
cite no comment whatever. But in Washington, the
Mecca toward which thousands flocked during the
war, and have continued to come ever since, one
finds all the peculiarities, habits, and language of the
negro of the slave period.

Their condition is somewhat improved in the majority of cases, but very many live in miserable cab-
ins or shanties, and crowd into them in such large
numbers, they seem much more like bees in a hive

than human beings. Others in better circumstances
have comfortable houses, are well clothed, and apparently quite prosperous.

Then, again, there is a still higher class, who live
in fine houses, and surround themselves with the
luxuries and refinements of life. They dress in the
latest style, attend influential churches, frequent the
concert, lecture, and theatre, and in every way seem
to be quite the equal of the white people.

It is in the first-named class though that we find
the traits and characteristics of the real negro. It is
also the largest class.

Both men and women are ignorant, stupid, super-
stitious, indolent, and improvident to a remarkable
degree. Give one a dollar and he will immediately
walk to the nearest market and invest part of it in
some expensive article of food and the remainder in
some flashy article of dress, never thinking nor car-
ing if any more dollars are to come to him on the
morrow, or ever again. Numbers of the women are
employed as servants in families, by the day—that
is, they go to the house of their employer in the
morning and return to their own contracted rooms
and houses at night. This kind of service has had
a tendency to induce pilfering in a small way. I

have observed it is almost the invariable custom among them to carry a basket or a bundle, and upon leaving at night for their homes, this basket or bundle is generally well freighted. Many remarkable developments have been made by suspicious housekeepers insisting upon an examination of the basket.

Their churches and societies — for every negro belongs either to a church or a society—are objects of affection and solicitude. These societies are beneficial and have really done much good. By paying a trifle each month towards the general fund, the members are entitled to $3 per week in case of sickness, and a decent burial in case of death—and it is just here the Washington negro is in his glory—if there is any one thing he dotes upon more than another, it is a funeral, a real first-class funeral !—with flowers, music, and carriages, and a long uniformed train of the members of his " 'ciety."

These funerals usually take place on Sunday, and it is a great disappointment if the demise of a brother occurs on a Monday or Tuesday, making it impossible to postpone the last sad rites to the next Sunday, and so have an opportunity for the beloved display.

The evening service at their churches rarely begins

Sabbath evenings before nine o'clock, and it is well on to ten and sometimes eleven o'clock before they are well warmed up "and in the spirit." They enjoy their freedom too well to give heed to the nine o'clock bell, which still tolls each night as it did twenty-five years ago, to summon the slaves to their respective homes.

I was returning home one evening from rather a protracted service at one of the fashionable churches in the upper part of the city, and happened to pass by one of these colored churches where the meeting was in full blast. I paused some time on the sidewalk and listened to what was going on within. The door was wide open, guarded by a colored deacon, and the little building crowded to its utmost capacity. The sable minister was praying in a loud tone, the words coming so strong and so fast it was impossible to understand one word he said, but his hearers inside evidently understood him, for several females were shouting vigorously, and at short intervals would utter a piercing shriek. It was just such a scene as I once witnessed years ago among the slaves in a Southern State.

The negro is ubiquitous in Washington. Start a brass band from the Capitol, and there will not be three taps upon the drum before a horde of colored men, women, and children will surround it and will follow all day if it continues to play.

Upon public occasions they take possession of the sidewalks, and, in their eagerness to see and hear, press forward so persistently that nothing short of a battery loaded with grape-shot could make any impression upon them.

If a circus comes to town—but here words fail me, to describe the delight, enjoyment, and golden opportunities the average negro manages to procure from the show.

They are very social in their nature and are also very loquacious, and the amount of visiting done by them and the talk that naturally follows, is somewhat astonishing.

If you have a servant in your kitchen you may safely count upon her receiving half-a-dozen calls every day, and the number of relatives she possesses outnumbers the "cousins" of Bridget two to one.

The old-fashioned forms of address, such as "Uncle," "Aunt," and "Mammy," once used by the negroes to each other, and by the younger members of the family where they were employed—have entirely disappeared, and the more formal terms of

"Mr.," "Mrs.," and "Miss" are adhered to with as much punctiliousness as in the highest circles of good society. To use the former style now might cause some awkward mistakes—as was the case with a young lady one day at the Capitol. She had been waiting some time in the reception-room, trying to send a note to a Senator on the floor, but had not been successful in doing so. Seeing a very genteel, benevolent-looking colored man going in the direction of the Senate Chamber, she impulsively called to him, "Uncle! will you be kind enough to give this note to Senator ——?" He bowed politely, smiled, and said he would. She was somewhat disconcerted, when she learned a few minutes later, she had called upon Senator Bruce to perform the service.

I have been very much interested in learning where the old slave "pens" were located, and found, upon questioning quite a number of persons, that not one in fifty could give me any idea whatever of their locality, although they had lived in the city, many of them thirty or forty years; showing that the trade in human chattels was such an ordinary every-day business that they did not know nor care where carried on.

4

After many inquiries I finally learned that the largest "pen" was on Eighth Street Southwest, between B and C Streets. The dwelling occupied by the trader at the time is still standing, but has been so changed and improved it bears no resemblance whatever to the former roughcast, yellow-washed farmhouse of thirty years ago. The spot where the "pen" actually stood, is now covered by a palatial residence, the property of a Methodist clergyman.

Selling slaves in the District of Columbia was prohibited in the year 1850, but the "pens" continued in existence right along up to the beginning of the war. An old slave told me he had seen as many as seventy-five slaves taken out at once from the pen on Eighth Street, chained together and marched down to the boat to be taken to Alexandria to be sold. Sometimes they would be taken just across the Long Bridge ; and frequently, to evade the law, to Bladensburg.

Slavery was abolished in the District by act of Congress of April 16, 1862, and $1,000,000 appropriated to reimburse the owners for their loss. Before obtaining the money, though, the owner was obliged to furnish proof of his loyalty, and the slave was required to go to the City Hall to be appraised by Commissioners appointed for the purpose. An eye-witness of the scenes around the City Hall at that time relates many amusing and touching incidents. Each slave was questioned closely as to what kind of labor he was capable of performing, in order to ascertain his value. In their eagerness to appear to as much advantage, and to be appraised as high as possible, they gave many quaint and laughable answers.

There are at present nearly sixty thousand negroes in the District, the most distinguished of whom, of course, is Mr. Frederick Douglas. The whole history of this remarkable man reads more like romance than real life, and one needs to see him in the flesh to be convinced there is really such a personage. He is extremely venerable in appearance, dignified in manner, and possesses fine conversational powers. Mr. Douglas finds little congeniality with the people of his own race, and enjoys the society of his white brethren far more than that of his own color.

The morality, or rather the want of it, among the colored people is attracting much attention at present. They have not advanced as rapidly as was hoped for, after being firmly set upon their feet in the way of education and self-improvement, and there is opportunity and need for much missionary work among them.

They are quite as imitative as the Chinese, but, unfortunately, imitate the vices and foibles of the whites rather than their virtues. They have an inordinate love of dress and finery, and will leave no stone unturned in their efforts to procure it. The appearance of some of the younger women rigged out in sheer muslins, dainty laces, and sweeping plumes, regardless of neatness or appropriateness, is sometimes a perfect burlesque upon the costume of a fashionable city belle.

VI.

January, 1881.

MRS. HAYES is a charming hostess and welcomes visitors to the White House with cordiality and grace. There is a pleasant Western heartiness in her greeting which impresses one very much with her sincerity, and makes you feel you are the invited expected guest instead of a curious visitor. This afternoon she held her first reception for the season, and was assisted by Mrs. Secretary Evarts, Mrs. Secretary Sherman, and several young ladies from distant States.

Mrs. Hayes was very tastefully attired in a rich black silk dress, *en traine*, and trimmed with jet *passementerie*—the neck cut V-shape and filled in with soft Spanish lace. In her glossy black hair was a silver comb.

Mrs. Evarts was richly dressed in black velvet. Mrs. Sherman wore an old gold satin petticoat with a waist and court train of black velvet. Her costume was brightened by a bouquet de corsage of red roses.

I wandered for some time through the conservatory enjoying the fragrance of the violets and heliotropes, and quietly noting the distinguished guests passing to and fro; among them were Sir Edward Thornton and Lady Thornton, and the Japanese Minister and wife, M. and Madame Yoshida. The latter was quite fashionably attired in a brown silk dress, seal-skin sacque, and a velvet bonnet with a bunch of bright flowers nestled under the brim. Both she and her husband have long since discarded the native dress.

Being the 8th of January and the anniversary of the battle of New Orleans, the full-length portrait of General Jackson—occupying a conspicuous place in the centre corridor—was beautifully trimmed with white and crimson camelias and festoons of a rare and delicate fern.

Mrs. Hayes makes a point of noticing the children who come to call upon her, and the little ones are always delighted with the attention, and innocently imagine the lovely hostess would be greatly disappointed if they failed to come.

This afternoon a friend of mine, accompanied by her little son, after being presented to Mrs. Hayes was about to pass on, thinking it useless to introduce the child also; but Mrs. Hayes was not to be put off in that way, and turning to the child, extended her hand and smilingly said, " Well, my little fellow, did you too come to my reception ?" He returned her salutation, evidently very much pleased, but did not say anything. When they were outside of the mansion he turned to his mother with a beaming face and very *naively* remarked, " Mamma, Mrs. Hayes was real glad I came to her reception this afternoon, wasn't she?"

VII.

IT was the favorite amusement of a celebrated
writer to sit by a window at the eventide on
one of the crowded thoroughfares of London and
watch the passing throng hurrying to their respective homes. Tales of woe, joy, gladness, hope,
sorrow, and fear could be read upon the different
faces as plainly as if written there in bold characters. Princes of the blood, nobles, careworn merchants, happy youth, fashion, and old age passed
rapidly before him, each proving an interesting
theme for his facile pen. The streets of Washington, though entirely different from a London scene,
are quite as interesting.

There are no princes, no nobility, no millionaire
merchants I admit; but there are distinguished men,
fair women, youth, beauty, sorrow, and suffering to

be seen; for human nature is very much the same everywhere.

Take Pennsylvania Avenue some bright, pleasant winter afternoon, and probably the very first person you will meet is a distinguished Senator or Member who has been making the halls of the Capitol ring with his eloquence, and whose speech, while he walks, is being flashed over the wires from city to city and town to town throughout the country; and yet he is going quietly to his home in as plain matter-of-fact way as yonder weary laborer returning from his day's toil.

Here comes a fine lady, attired in a rich velvet dress most elaborately trimmed. A handsome mantle covers her shoulders and a fashionable hat graces her tossing head. The complacent air with which she walks is amusing, and more so when it is known the dress is entirely new to her. She is the wife of a Western politician, and in her far-off country home her best gown was nothing better than plain cashmere, and jewels she never thought of wearing, but "when at Rome do as Romans do," and as everybody in her circle wears fine clothes, she should do the same, and what does it matter if the style is a

little overdrawn? she is satisfied, and others should
be as well.

Right behind her is a tall, slender lady with a pale,
sad face; her dress is of the cheapest kind, but the
spotless collar and cuffs, the air of quiet refinement
proclaim the real lady. Her history is touching—
do you care to hear it? The daughter of a brilliant
man, who once made his mark in public life, she was
at one time the pet and joy of a bright, happy home.
A turn of the wheel of fortune deprived the father
of wealth, and death soon after claiming him for a
victim, there was nothing left for the daughter but
to take up the burden of life for herself and widowed
mother. She procured a clerkship in one of the Departments, and has faithfully performed the duties;
but being "only a woman" her salary is very small,
and the struggle to make one salary do the work of
two for the little household has paled the cheek and
saddened the brow.

What a marked contrast in the young man walking so leisurely twirling a cane and puffing a fragrant cigar! He, too, is a clerk, but you would
never think so, for the "nobby" suit, delicate gloves,
and air of fashion indicate a man of leisure and
means. He might be taken for the son of a million-

aire, or probably an attaché of a foreign legation, and if strangers were told he is only a Government clerk on a salary of $1200 a year, they would imagine Washington a paradise for poor people, where so much style can be supported upon so small an income. But they do not know of the unpaid bills and cool assurance of this young man, or they would understand it all.

A carriage dashes past; in it is seated a beautiful woman; the lovely complexion, hazel eyes, and soft waving hair are fair to look upon; the rich India shawl, thrown so carelessly about her, and the creamy white bonnet exceedingly becoming. She is the wife of a young and rising Member, and tasting the sweets of Washington life—which to an ambitious woman are so delightful. What the end will be no one can tell, but history is constantly repeating itself, and the past has revealed the happy, loving young wife, after ten years of fashionable life at the Capital, transformed from the gentle, domestic woman into the vain frivolous creature of society. This lady has plunged into the whirlpool, and Fashion has no more faithful devotee.

Any number of *bonnes* are to be seen in jaunty aprons and ruffled caps, wheeling handsome little

carriages with bright-eyed, rosy-cheeked occupants;
and the amusing part, not one in ten are French,
but either first saw the light in Erin's Emerald Isle
or "away down in Dixie" among the cotton fields,
rice plantations, and canebrakes.

The novel spectacle of a Chinese of high rank in
his native dress walking the streets surrounded by a
crowd of ragged negro boys, would create a sensation in any other city, but the sight is such a common one on Pennsylvania Avenue it excites nothing
more than a smile.

Now comes the " office-seeker," one of the peculiarities of the streets of Washington. We meet
him at every turn—around the steps and doors of
the hotel, in the Departments, at the Capitol—he is
everywhere; and it is sad to see the eagerness with
which he clutches every ray of hope. He implicitly
believes all promises made him, and remains day
after day, week after week, waiting for the anticipated vacancy, until his money is all spent, his
credit gone, and at last very often obliged to return
home no nearer the promised appointment than
when he came to the city.

Sorrow and suffering are not absent from the
streets of the Capital, but they are presented in less

pitiable forms than in other cities. The streets are wide, and there are so many parks one is not brought in such close contact with the masses as in New York, Philadelphia, and other places: suffering and destitution viewed from a distance do not assume the same proportions as when crowded under our eyes.

VIII.

THERE are quite a number of interesting private residences located in various parts of the city, which may be termed historical houses; and one need take only an occasional walk with some old resident to learn all about them. Some of them were erected about the same time the foundations of the Capitol were laid. Others were once the abode of distinguished individuals and influential families, and several the scene of violence and blood. Time has been very busy with many of them, and their former beauty and grandeur have departed forever. This is particularly true of the famous old *Van Ness* mansion, situated at the foot of Seventeenth Street, by the Potomac River.

Daniel Burns was one of the original proprietors of the land now occupied by the city, and its importance and growth brought him a fortune from the sale of building lots. John P. Van Ness, a member of Congress from New York, married his only daughter, Marcia, who at her father's death inherited the fortune. With this money Mr. Van Ness erected the mansion referred to, which was considered very grand and elegant at that time.

It is a spacious square building, with fine verandas across the front, and when new had many conveniences and adornments, not found in other houses of the city. There were ample grounds around it, filled with trees and shrubbery, beds of gay flowers and trailing vines. The garden in front was terraced down to the water's edge. Music, feasting, and dancing were a part of Southern hospitality in those days, and this roof had many merry parties gathered beneath it, where the young and old mingled in the giddy dance and enjoyed the hospitality of the courtly owner.

But everything is very much changed now. The mansion is fast going to decay, the trees gnarled and unshapely, the shrubbery rank and overgrown in some places, and in others broken down entirely. The flowers and bordered walks are all gone, and the pretty terraced garden an unsightly wilderness and rapidly becoming a swamp. Worse than the

ruin, though, staring one in the face, the fact that
the premises are now used as an ice-cream saloon
and summer-garden for negroes, and those of not
the most reputable character either. Just think of
it! the mansion so costly and once so famous, transformed into a summer-garden for negroes!

"Duddington," on Capitol Hill, is another very
old mansion, and quite as aristocratic as the above.
It is the old home of Daniel Carroll, a near relative
of Charles Carroll of "Carrollton."   The spacious
hall, lofty pillars, and polished floors were modelled
after the style of old English mansions, and the
grounds were extensive and handsome. The master
delighted in receiving and entertaining beneath his
roof the first men of the nation, and was noted for
the dignity and stateliness of his manners.   The
family are all gone now, and very little of the former
glory of the place remaining.

There are three bright, attractive houses opposite
the east park of the Capitol and commanding a fine
view of the grounds, which are at present the quiet
homes of three prominent families. These houses
have a look of such substantial comfort, one would
never dream of there having been so many weary
days and hopeless nights passed within them, nor of

the tales of woe whispered to, and echoed back from, the solid walls. The building—it was originally all in one—has a history, for it is no other than the "Old Capitol Prison;" which name, to many now living, is synonymous with suffering, darkness, and despair. During the war hundreds of prisoners were confined there, and an execution once took place in the yard. Congress held its sessions there before occupying the present Capitol, and the building was then made into two private residences, and kept as boarding-houses for a number of years. Many distinguished men of both Houses of Congress made their home there during the sessions, and John C. Calhoun died there.

At the corner of Lafayette Place and "H" Street stands a house around which are clustered historic memories; it is the old home of one who at one time was the nation's idol, and who breathed his last within its walls. I refer to Commodore Decatur. The house was built by him, and the most distinguished men of the nation were in the habit of visiting there.

The whole history of the duel between Decatur and Barron, which resulted in his death, is very sad, and throws a dark cloud over the brilliant record of each.

5

I presume every one is familiar with the story of
the unfortunate affair of the English ship-of-war
" Leopard" and the American frigate "Chesapeake,"
commanded by Commodore Barron, and how the
latter was accused of neglect of duty in failing to
have his guns in readiness to meet the enemy, and
therefore obliged to surrender the "Chesapeake,"
firing one gun as she struck her colors. A court-
martial for this affair followed, and he was suspended
for five years. Great effort was made by some to
have him reinstated; others strongly opposed such
action—among them Commodore Decatur. This
greatly incensed Commodore Barron, and, after a
sharp correspondence had passed between them, he
sent Decatur a challenge, which was accepted; and
the duel fought near Bladensburg, March 22, 1820,
resulted in the latter falling mortally wounded.

He was carried home, where in a few hours he
expired. His death cast a gloom over the whole
city, and a "drawing-room" to be held that evening
at the White House was postponed in consequence.

The funeral was very imposing, and minute guns
were fired from the Navy Yard while the procession
was passing from the house to the place of inter-
ment.

The house—a very handsome one—was afterward occupied by various prominent persons, among them Judah P. Benjamin, who furnished it in the most luxurious manner, and brought his young French wife there. Mr. Benjamin, as is well known, became the Secretary of State of the Southern Confederacy, and later, quite eminent as Queen's Councillor in England.

General Beale is the present occupant, and entertains in the most lavish manner. General and Mrs. Grant usually stay with him during their brief visits to Washington.

Another very interesting house on "H" Street is that known as the Freeman House. It is directly opposite Lafayette Square, and was the abode of Lord Ashburton during his important mission to America. All readers of history understand the importance of the "Ashburton Treaty," and how it settled forever certain differences between England and the United States by defining the boundary lines of Maine and Canada.

The house was built, or rather commenced, by a gentleman who became financially embarrassed before fully completed, and who was very glad to rent it to the distinguished foreigner for £1000 per annum.

Lord Ashburton was a plain matter-of-fact sort of man, and one of his eccentricities was to carry an immense green silk umbrella, to protect him from the sun or the rain. There is a fine portrait of his lordship in the State Department.

Not quite a square from the above-named mansion and in full view of it is the Seward House, which has been made historical by two events. Secretary Seward was living there the night he received the wounds from a would-be assassin; when a pall, as it were, fell over the whole city, and men held their breath with fear, and neighbor dared not trust his neighbor; and Philip Barton Key received his death wound from the hand of General Sickles while standing within a few feet of the front door. At the time this last event occurred the house was used as a club-house, and Key was in the habit of spending much of his time there.

Indeed, almost every house around Lafayette Square has some interesting story, or been the abode at one time of some distinguished personage. The old home of Charles Sumner faces the park, and the present residence of W. W. Corcoran also. The latter, quite an old house, was rented by Daniel Webster when Secretary of State. He was always very lavish in his expenditures, and gave many elegant dinners and other entertainments during his residence there. After Mr. Corcoran purchased it, and during the late war, it was occupied by M. Montholon, the French Minister, who also entertained very handsomely.

Mr. Corcoran has occupied the house a number of years, and many improvements have been added, so that it is now one of the finest in the city. There is a large garden in the rear filled with flowers and shrubbery and choice fruit trees.

On Highland Place above Fourteenth Street stands quite an old house, built by Secretary Crawford. When completed, it was the finest and almost the only one in that immediate neighborhood—all beyond it was open country. But everything is very much changed. Beautiful mansions have sprung up all around and several squares beyond. Wealth and culture are visible upon all sides. The equestrian statue of General Thomas is within a few rods of it and the Louise Home almost directly opposite.

Secretary Crawford was a somewhat remarkable character in his day. At one time he ran for the Presidency. In 1807 he ran for Senator in Georgia and had an exciting canvass, managed to fight two duels during that time, killing his opponent in the first and being wounded himself in the second.

He was Minister to France at one time, and a warm friend of Lafayette, who made him his agent for his American lands. He is said to have been of a social disposition, enjoyed having his friends visit him, and his house was known in the family as Liberty Hall.

On Tenth Street, directly opposite the Medical Museum, is the house in which Abraham Lincoln breathed his last. It is a plain, unpretending mansion, but made interesting by the sad scenes of that event.

The Octagon House, corner of New York Avenue and Eighteenth Street, is one of the most celebrated houses in Washington. It is of peculiar design, as the name indicates, and was originally very elegant and stylish. It was built about 1798 by Colonel John Tayloe, one of the rich men of the District, who entertained in princely style.

After the burning of the White House, in 1814, President and Mrs. Madison went there to live, and the New-Year's reception of 1815 was held there. The Treaty of Ghent is said to have been signed in this house, and the President received and entertained many distinguished visitors from other countries. It is now very much out of repair, and, moreover, said to be haunted, and rarely ever occupied. Whether the ghost is a Presidential one or only a "commoner," I have not learned.

There seems to be a strange fatality about many fine residences of the city. Houses, once the homes of wealthy, prominent men, and the place where beauty and fashion were wont to mingle in social intercourse, are now closed or degenerated into that much-abused institution, "a Washington boarding house." And this has not been brought about, as frequently happens in other cities, by the death of the head of the family, the march of trade or demands of fashion pointing to more desirable localities, for many are on quiet streets, and many in fashionable neighborhoods. It seems to be due rather to the changeable nature of the population. Every four years new men come to the front, and many launch out into an extravagant style of living; and if by chance they continue in public positions longer than the four years, begin to imagine their sojourn in Washington permanent, and rear for themselves fine mansions, gather luxuries and comforts about them, and in a flash the political wheel makes a turn, leaving them without position and frequently without money. Then the home is broken up, the household lares and penates become scattered; the house passes into the hands of strangers, and in time the ubiquitous white card hangs by the door.

"Kalorama," located on the hills near Rock Creek, outside of the city limits, may also be called one of the historical houses of Washington. It was built in 1805 by Joel Barlow, a poet and politician, and, moreover, a shrewd business man. Having amassed a fortune in France by successful speculations, he returned to America to enjoy it. Washington was chosen as the place for his future home, and he erected this elegant mansion, laid out the grounds in fine style, filled them with fountains and statuary, and opened his door to his friends. It seems he did not enjoy his handsome residence very long, for in 1811 he accepted the position of Minister to France, and, while abroad, when travelling in Poland, contracted a heavy cold and died in a cottage near Cracow.

The mansion has had many different occupants since then, and, like many other old residences around the city, could tell strange tales of joy, sorrow, and ambition, if endowed with the power of speech.

There is an old vault• on the place in which the remains of Decatur were placed at the time of his death, and where they remained until the year 1846, when they were removed to Philadelphia.

———————

Near Bladensburg is another fine old mansion, known as " Riversdale." Very many persons suppose this to be the old family residence of the Lords Baltimore, as it was the home of a Calvert; this, however, is not the case. Their seat was at Mount Airy, Md., and the title became extinct with Frederick, the sixth Lord Baltimore. Having the misfortune to lose his wife shortly after marriage, he became very profligate, went abroad, and died when quite a young man. The Calverts of Riversdale must have descended from another branch of the family. The mansion was built, or rather commenced, by a wealthy gentleman from Belgium. He had a very pretty daughter, and Mr. Calvert being caught in the toils of Cupid, succeeded in winning her hand. After they were married he completed the house and resided there with his wife.

The mansion is about a hundred years old and after the style of an Italian villa. The rooms are large and the ceilings very high.. The grounds were formerly very handsome and well stocked with deer; and all the surroundings in accord with the generous style of living of the owner. Many distinguished men from Washington were in the habit of visiting there during the lifetime of the late Charles Calvert, Esq., and Henry Clay wrote the Missouri Compromise bill under this roof.

IX

CORCORAN ART GALLERY.

PHILADELPHIA was fortunate in having a Girard, and Baltimore a Peabody, to remember them in the distribution of a fortune. Washington has been quite as fortunate in having a Corcoran. The latter has preferred to bestow his gifts during his lifetime, so that he has double pleasure thereby; pleasure in giving away large sums of money, and pleasure in seeing the good results flowing therefrom and in knowing it has been properly applied to the purpose intended.

The city is indebted to him for the beautiful building at the corner of Seventeenth Street and Pennsylvania Avenue known as the Corcoran Art Gallery; which was deeded to the Trustees May 10, 1869, "for the encouragement of Painting, Sculpture, and the Fine Arts," with the condition that "it should be open to visitors without charge two days in the week, and on other days at moderate and reasonable charges," the latter to be applied to the current expenses of preserving and keeping in order the building and its contents.

The building is of brick in the Renaissance style, with brown-stone facings and ornaments. It fronts on Pennsylvania Avenue 106 feet, and runs back on Seventeenth Street 125 feet.

The front is of imposing style, divided by pilasters, having capitals of the Columbian style representing Indian corn, into recesses, four stone niches for statues, with trophies and wreaths of foliage finely carved, the monogram of the founder, and the inscription " Dedicated to Art."

The niches intended for the reception of statues have been nearly all filled. Those across the front containing respectively Phidias, Raphael, Michael Angelo, and Albert Durer, representing the sister arts of Sculpture, Painting, Engraving, and Architecture. They are seven feet high and are carved from fine Carrara marble. The niches on the side contain statues of Titian, Rubens, Rembrandt, and Da Vinci.

The building is two stories in height. The first

floor is devoted to sculpture, bronzes, and ceramics. The second floor contains the Picture galleries.

The main Picture Gallery is ninety-five feet long by forty-four feet wide, and lighted from the roof. The walls are of a maroon tint, and the ceilings frescoed and gilded. The cost of the building and ground was $250,000. Mr. Corcoran placed his private collection of pictures and statuary in it, valued at $100,000 more. There is an endowment fund of $900,000, yielding an annual income of $60,000.

Ascending the broad stairway leading to the Picture galleries, the first picture to meet the eye is a very fine portrait of the donor of this treasure-house—W. W. Corcoran, Esq. It was painted some years ago by Charles L. Elliott, who died a year or two after completing it. It is considered an excellent likeness. There are a few notable pictures in the gallery by celebrated artists, and some very good ones by artists not so well known. The portraits are particularly interesting.

Church's Niagara occupies a conspicuous place, and is to me the gem of the collection. To look upon this picture when the sun is shining brightly over head, is the next best thing to standing beside the mighty cataract. The mist is there, the beautiful rainbow, the vast volume of vivid green water, the boiling and rushing rapids, the distant trees in their autumn foliage—everything but the strange, solemn roar—what a great pity the artist could not transfer that also to his canvas! I have heard $12,000 was the price paid for it, and I am sure the sum is moderate, considering the pleasure that twelve thousand people have had in looking at it, many of whom will never have an opportunity of beholding the reality.

Another beautiful picture is "Charlotte Corday in Prison." It was painted by Muller, an eminent French artist, and came directly from his hand to the gallery. The pale, sad face looking through the prison bars is strangely fascinating. It has been extensively copied, as is well known, and photographs of it are sold by hundreds.

The French picture, "Le Regiment qui Passe," by Detaille, representing a regiment of soldiers passing through the streets of Paris on a wet, snowy day, is very fine.

"Mount Corcoran," by Bierstadt, is also good. "Edict of William the Testy," by Boughton, is an interesting picture. It was painted expressly for this gallery, and the artist received a handsome compensation. Another very beautiful and curious picture is the "Procession of the Sacred Bull Apis-Osiris," by Bridgman.

The side galleries leading from the main hall to the Octagon Room contain a number of portraits, principally of the Presidents and Vice-Presidents.

In the centre of the Octagon Room, which has been lined with maroon cashmere, is Powers's Greek Slave, beautiful enough in itself to need no framing of color and light, but still more beautiful in contrast with the dark, rich color around it. A few choice busts have been honored with a place in the same room.

The Hall of Sculpture contains a few pieces of marble, but the principal part of the collection consists of plaster casts of celebrated statues, at present in the Vatican, Louvre, British Museum, and the Museums of Florence and Naples. Of course, like the originals, many of them are in a mutilated condition, and as the gallery is visited daily by many persons who never heard of Venus, Apollo, Iris, and other mythological personages, there is often much wonderment expressed at their condition. A rural visitor one day, unable to restrain her surprise, was overheard to say, "I do wonder how all them things got broke!"

The collection of bronzes and ceramics, although not large, is valuable and beautiful. A number of choice articles were added at the close of the Centennial Exhibition; Mr. Corcoran purchased them for this purpose.

A large Japanese bowl three feet in diameter, decorated with serpents and dragons, which attracted much attention in the Main Building at Philadelphia, is now in the gallery. Also two vases and a square table in Cloisonné, three hundred years old; and a bronze Japanese Yoshitaure vase.

There are three very fine "Arita" porcelain Japanese vases made expressly for the Centennial Exhibition and of unusual size and finish.

The electrotype reproductions of the "Hildesheim Treasures" are very interesting; also those of other articles at present in the British Museum.

X.

PRESIDENT GARFIELD.

March 4, 1881.

THE inauguration of President Garfield at the Capitol this morning was a very different affair from the inauguration of his predecessor four years ago.

A slight fall of snow yesterday somewhat marred the preparations for the day, but did not seriously interfere with them, for the sun came out warm and bright at an early hour, and by the time the last division of troops taking part in the pageant had passed in review the streets were perfectly dry.

The arrangements for handling and marching such a large body of men were excellent, and everything moved on as easily and quietly as any .one could wish for.

The scene upon Pennsylvania Avenue, as the President and President-elect passed down on their way to the Capitol, has never before been equalled

6

in Washington. A triumphal arch had been erected
between the Treasury Building and the building
opposite, and tastefully decorated with flags and
streamers and the coat-of-arms of the various States.
The Treasury, from pavement to roof, was a mass of
evergreens, flags, and streamers. Every public building along the route was decorated in a similar manner, and the owners of private residences seemed to
vie with each other as to which should belong the
honor of having the most elaborate adornment.

The passage down was a perfect ovation from beginning to end ; a sea of heads surged upon the sidewalk and filled all the windows and roofs of the
houses along the route.

An equally enthusiastic audience met the distinguished party at the Capitol, and the scenes there
were both interesting and impressive.

The short time spent in returning from the Capitol
to the White House I think must have been the
proudest moments in Mr. Garfield's life. He is the
lawfully inaugurated President of the great American
people, has reached the highest position possible for
man to reach in this country, and the plaudits and
greetings which burst from ten thousand throats
seemed to indicate entire satisfaction in the result.

At the Treasury Department, as the open carriage with its four prancing gray horses turned to enter the south gate leading to the Executive Mansion, the enthusiasm was so great that Mr. Garfield felt obliged to acknowledge it, and standing erect in the carriage, uncovered his head, and bowed repeatedly in response to the hearty greeting. He would have been more than mortal not to have felt a thrill of triumph at that moment.

July 4, 1881.

What a remarkable country this is, and how rapidly events follow each other, keeping one in a perpetual state of excitement! A dark cloud has settled over this fair city, and indeed may be said to extend over the whole land. Yesterday the city was radiant with inaugural festivities; to-day all is dark, gloomy, uncertain! The President has been stricken down by the hand of an assassin, and no one can foretell the result.

I stood, on Saturday morning last, on the same spot where I was standing the 4th day of March, as the newly made President rose in his carriage, bowed to the cheering multitude, and was whirled in through the south gate leading to the Executive Mansion, but oh! what a contrast! There were no holiday decorations; no gay banners and streamers floating out in the morning breeze; no strains of martial music filling the air; no cheering multitude, and no handsome barouche drawn by four prancing gray steeds. Instead of these, I saw an ambulance turn in the gate; before it three mounted policemen, and as many more in the rear. A carriage slowly followed, and a crowd of ragged, curious negroes came close behind. The latter were shut out at the gate, and the mournful procession moved slowly to the door, where an anxious group awaited its arrival. The wounded man raised his hand when he saw his friends, but could not speak.

This is usually a day of great rejoicing here, but no one has any heart for gayety; even the boys who look forward to the day with so much pleasure have abstained from their accustomed amusements.

I stopped for a few moments at the White House gate, about sunset, to learn the latest tidings from the sick chamber. Groups were standing all along the square waiting for the same purpose. High and low were there, and each seemed equally interested. The grounds look strangely picturesque with the white tents of the soldiers scattered over them, and

an armed sentinel pacing to and fro before each
gate. The sufferings of the distinguished patient
have touched a chord in every breast, and the sympathy apparently perfectly sincere.

September.

If the contrast between the journey of the President on March 4th and July 2d was very great, I
think the early morning ride of yesterday greater
still. Lifted from his couch by tender and loving
hands, laid upon a mattress in an express wagon,
and driven slowly down the avenue, in the dull morning light of the hour between daybreak and sun-
rise; no one visible upon the streets except a
laborer here and there hastening to his distant place
of daily toil, or a marketman starting out upon his
daily round; the patient slowly, slowly dying, and
longing, longing for a sight of the sea. Could anything be more touching or more sad? The President has longed so much to go to the sea-shore that
his physicians decided to gratify him, and the preparations for the journey were begun some days ago.
It is astonishing what deep interest has been taken
in these preparations by all classes.

In order to avoid driving over rough cobble-stones

to the car, the railroad company kindly ordered a branch track laid up to the very edge of the concrete pavement on Pennsylvania Avenue, so that the sick man could be lifted directly from the wagon, which carried him on a mattress to the station, into the car.   After the preparations were completed the spot was visited by hundreds of men, women, and children, eager to inspect them and look into the car in which the distinguished sufferer was to ride. The journey was successfully made, and the news to-day encourages the hope that he may yet recover.

September 23.

Pennsylvania Avenue is clothed to-day in the habiliments of mourning.   With muffled drums, measured steps, and bowed heads, the people have paid the last sad honors to James A. Garfield.

February 1, 1882.

This is the beginning of the fourth month of the trial of the assassin Guiteau, and it is so interminable that one feels like flying away from the city to some obscure corner, where it would be impossible to hear or read anything more about it.

Strange to say, refined, cultivated ladies have been visiting the court-room day after day, and have seemed to really enjoy the remarkable proceedings. This is one of the peculiar phases of Washington life. It would not be possible to induce these same ladies to attend the trial of a common murderer in New York or Boston, and yet they are willing to crowd into this court-room, suffer all sorts of discomforts, and listen to many things they ought not to hear—and for what? It is not any interest in the prisoner, nor sympathy for his relatives, nor the profound learning and wonderful eloquence of his counsel that attract them. I think one word will explain all, viz: Notoriety.

July 2.

Charles J. Guiteau, the wretched man, who by his dastardly act one year ago caused the death of a fellow man, and plunged the nation in a deep wave of sorrow, on Friday last paid the penalty of his crime, and another dark chapter in the history of the country has been closed.

XI

SOCIETY.

IT seems as though the Capitol should be the grand centre of national refinement, literature, and science, and that intelligent cultivated people should there find the society most congenial to them. This, however, is not the case. True, much culture may be found, also refinement and learning, and among the residents there are any number of distinguished authors and scientists; but the literary feature is not as conspicuous as in some other cities I could name, and is in constant danger of being overshadowed altogether by the glitter and show attending position and wealth.

Society, as at present existing in Washington, is very peculiarly made up, and at its best very hollow and unsatisfactory.

During the "season," which begins about the first of December and continues until the beginning of

Lent, there is one round of gayety. Receptions, balls, and other entertainments follow each other in rapid succession—frequently several occurring of an evening; and the guests flit from one house to another, spending an hour or more at each.

At these receptions Fashion reigns supreme, and the jewels and toilets of the ladies are costly and elegant.

The wives of prominent officials, including Cabinet officers, Judges of the Supreme Court, Speaker of the House of Representatives, and Senators and Members, have certain hours one day each week, during the season, for receiving their friends. But the receptions are not confined to friends, for their houses are, in a certain sense, open to the public, and any one of presentable appearance can walk in and pay his or her "respects," introducing himself if necessary, partake of a cup of coffee or chocolate, and enjoy a chat with the hostess if so inclined.

There is often a great crowd and the hostess is usually assisted by several lady friends, to whom you are introduced in succession. If your name happens to be an uncommon one, or very long, by the time you reach the last lady in the line, it becomes so much distorted you would not recognize it yourself, and of course it is impossible for strangers to ; consequently, if you meet these same ladies again, more than likely they will not remember your face and do not know your correct name, therefore you have to be introduced a second and sometimes a third time.

These receptions in course of time become a great bore to the ladies receiving, and they are generally very glad when the season is over.

Society is very much broken up into " sets" or "cliques." The individuals making up the one set affiliate with those composing the others, but the distinctive set still remains. For example, there is the army and navy set, which prides itself upon its exclusiveness, and rather inclines to the opinion that it represents the aristocracy of the country. There is also the official and congressional set, conspicuous only during a session of Congress. Then, again, there is a literary set, made up of authors, newspaper correspondents, and book-worms generally. Then, too, there is a musical set, composed of musical societies, professors of music, and amateurs of every degree of proficiency.

The custom of keeping "open house" one day each week, by the families of officials, gives many persons a chance of "getting into society," who could not if they were obliged to depend upon an invitation. During the winter time Washington is filled with a floating population of strangers, many of whom are adventurers and persons of no standing and frequently of no reputation in their former homes; many do not possess a dollar in the world, except what they pick up from day to day by their wits. Their stock in trade, if females, consists very often of nothing more than one or two attractive costumes, a fair face, and a great deal of assurance. They live, or rather lodge, in cheap lodging-houses, and depend upon the reception or afternoon "tea" to furnish them at least one good meal each day, the others they very often do without. They cultivate the acquaintance of Members and Senators, and sometimes, under favorable circumstances, entertain them at supper or whist, and in return ask political favors in the most unblushing manner. This class find Washington a most delightful place for a winter's sojourn, and if the veil could be lifted which obscures the true character of many of those crowding the parlors of officials upon reception days, I am very sure this description would apply to them.

The female lobbyist is nothing new in Washington; she was prominent half a century ago, and she

plies her trade quite as diligently to-day as she did
then. I clipped the following advertisement recently
from a morning journal, which I think proves this
assertion :—

PERSONAL.—A LADY WHO HAS BEEN SUCCESSFUL
in a quiet way of obtaining claims through congressional influence, will take charge of a good claim where the parties will pay a
retainer. Address, in confidence, "Sub Rosa," etc.

It is always more pleasant to dwell upon the fair
and beautiful side of life, than upon the dark and
unattractive; but I find it impossible for one to live
many years in Washington without discovering a
dark side; and that many things are tolerated in society which would be more in keeping with the state
of morals existing in the French capital under the
old *régime,* than what one has a right to look for in
the enlightened, purified society of republican America.   These evils may really not be any greater
than in other cities of the country, but Washington
labors under the disadvantage of being more public.
Everybody is so well known, and such publicity
given to private affairs, that that which in other
places is a mere ripple, confined to a narrow circle,
becomes in Washington a well developed breaker.

Vaulting ambition, frivolity, and reckless extravagance are some of the minor evils; there are others

of a more serious character. Intemperance prevails to an alarming extent, and, unfortunately, is not confined to the male sex.

Intrigue seems to flourish under the shadow of the dome, and social circles are constantly being startled by a tale of scandal. Some are uncharitable enough to say that this is owing to the presence of so many foreigners in the city; that they bring the peculiar notions of other lands regarding woman with them, and do not have the proper respect for the sex that Americans have. This may be true to a certain extent, but, alas! the foreign element forms a very small proportion of the so-called social circle, and therefore cannot be responsible for so much wrongdoing. They are more indifferent to public opinion than the Americans, and therefore more open in their transgressions. It has not been many years since one of them created a sensation in the city by reason of a piece of deception practised upon the unsuspecting, which caused considerable gossip at the time. The gentleman, an *attaché* of a foreign legation—secretary or something of the kind —was accompanied to this country by a dark-haired, dark-eyed lady, who was very beautiful and charming. She was not introduced into society, nor, in-

deed, ever seen in the city; but there were hints
constantly being dropped about a pretty little cottage in the suburbs where, amidst climbing roses
and sweet-scented honeysuckle, the fair lady awaited
the daily visits of the gallant secretary.

After a time the secretary was recalled to his own
country and the affair was almost forgotten in Washington.   In the course of time he again appeared in
the Capital, this time as the accredited Minister of a
powerful government, and was accompanied by his
wife, a beautiful lady with dark sparkling eyes and a
wealth of wonderful blonde hair.   She dressed with
exquisite taste, entertained charmingly, and was considered quite an acquisition to society.   The current
of life flowed on smoothly and pleasantly with the
pair, and no one supposed the lady had ever before
been in America.   At a dinner party one day, a
gentleman who had seen the beauty of the vine-clad
cottage, made the startling discovery that Madame
and the dark-eyed lady were one and the same
person!

There are many worshippers of Mammon to be
found in Washington, and the deference paid to pos-
sessors of wealth is truly lamentable.   Some persons
are living there now who, from their loose observ-

ance of the proprieties of life, have been disbarred from good society elsewhere, yet owing to their ability to make a stylish appearance and entertain handsomely, are recognized, and their shortcomings to a great extent overlooked.

The deference paid to gold is bad enough, but I think the toadyism existing much worse. It has no equal elsewhere, at least not in this country. It runs through every grade of society, and the obsequious court paid to influence and position is carried to such an extent it becomes an annoyance and an absurdity. This is particularly noticeable in the stores and other places of business. In Philadelphia, Baltimore, and other cities, one customer is waited upon with as much alacrity and politeness as another; but in Washington, if Mrs. Secretary Smith or Mrs. Chief Justice Jones drives up in her carriage, the ordinary customer must step aside and wait until they are served; or, if she insists upon being attended to first, it is done in such an ungracious manner, she is glad to escape from the place rather than suffer further humiliation.

Living in hotels and boarding-houses the whole or greater part of the year, as many families do, is to be deplored. It has a tendency to produce false ideas of life, and the effect must sooner or later be perceptible in the tone of society.

There is a spirit of emulation excited among the young people particularly, and the constant intercourse and intimate association with others of larger means induces extravagance and love of ease in those who cannot well afford it. Hotel life is an indolent one, to say the least, and a very unwholesome atmosphere in which to rear a family, as it does away with the innocent pleasures and restraints of the home circle, and opens the way for forming acquaintances who are often very undesirable. Girls become so accustomed, almost from infancy, to meeting strangers, they lose all shyness and reserve of manner, and long before they are grown have all the ease, repartee, and dissimulation of a fashionable woman. ·

And then, too, life in a hotel or boarding-house is so terribly unsatisfactory, it rather forces many into the whirlpool of dissipation who would not otherwise be drawn in. There are no home duties to be performed, no parlors to dust, no treasured china and silver to be washed after a cosey breakfast, no dainty cake or dessert to be prepared, no room to be made ready for the coming guest, and for whom the house

is to be "swept and garnished;" how are people to kill
the time of which they have such an abundant supply? The answer is to be found in the every-day
life of nine-tenths of the guests of every boarding-
house in the city.

After a late breakfast, they idle away an hour or
so in the public parlor, talk over the opera or ball, or
the last new dress; then an hour must be spent in
preparing for the promenade or morning call; after
that comes lunch, and again the toilet must be ad-
justed for the reception or afternoon "tea;" dinner
then occupies the time for another hour, and after
dinner the evening may be devoted to the theatre,
the German, the ball, or spent in the parlor in frivolous conversation. Is it not easy to see what effect
such a life must have upon those whose characters
are being formed?

It is hardly fair, though, to dwell so long upon the
shadow of the picture without calling attention to
the bright side, and I am happy to say there is a
bright side, pencilled in such vivid tints that the
whole is illumined.

There are very many charming homes where faithful husbands and loving wives are conscientiously and
religiously performing the duties of life and training

7

their little ones in the way they should go. There is a noble spirit of philanthropy abroad and no suffering cause ever appeals in vain for help.

In times of public calamity, such as famine, flood, or pestilence, the people are lavish in their contributions and thoroughly unselfish in their warm-hearted sympathy.

Struggling artists and authors find a hand ever ready to help them, and in no other place is there such a readiness to recognize talent of any kind. Even in the most fashionable houses and in the midst of a winter's round of gayety, some time is spared for " sweet charity." The Children's Hospital is a notable example of this. Beginning in a small room, rented for the purpose, it has grown to splendid proportions; and now relieves the sufferings and administers to the comforts of hundreds of children, in a large well-appointed building reared by the generosity of kind-hearted ladies and gentlemen.

Congress makes a small appropriation annually, but the greater part of the expense is borne by these persons. The Charity Ball, given each winter for the benefit of the hospital, is usually the most brilliant affair of the fashionable season.

The people are also remarkably hospitable, and it

must be acknowledged in very many things no other city is half so charming.

One very pleasing feature of the social life is the opportunity afforded for unexpected and pleasant meetings between acquaintances and friends.

So many persons drift to the Capital in pursuit of business or pleasure, that it has become a common saying, that "everybody turns up in Washington once in four years;" and in no other city could these romantic and remarkable meetings occur.

Young men have been known to leave homes in the East, to seek home and fortune in the far West, and after the lapse of many years found their way to the Capital as an honored representative of their adopted State, and surprised and pleased to find patrons and companions of their boyhood serving in Congress with them.

The experiences of the late war drew many persons together at times under peculiar circumstances, and the scenes and incidents attending them were often of such a character as to be almost impossible to forget them. To be brought face to face again after the lapse of many years is sometimes very pleasant and interesting.

A remarkable meeting of this kind occurred at

the White House a short time after the inauguration
of President Garfield. A number of friends were
spending the evening socially with Mrs. Garfield,
and among them Miss R——, a lady well known in
Washington. During the war she was very much
interested in the sick and wounded soldiers gathered
in hospitals in various parts of the city, and in the
habit of devoting two hours each day to them, allow-
ing nothing to interfere with her visits. In a hospital
on " I" Street, one morning, she found a young man
whose leg had just been amputated. The operation
had been a severe one and the bleeding very profuse.
Too weak to bear the taking up of the artery, the
only hope for his life was in having some one remain beside him with the finger pressed upon the
open artery. The father of the young man was
equal to the task, and by his devotion saved the life
of his son. Miss R—— paused at his bedside, spoke
cheering words, and finding she could not help him
passed on, thinking the case a hopeless one, and
that in a few hours more another name would be
added to the " roll of honor." She was called away
from the city the next morning, and lost sight of the
sufferers for a time, and, in the confusion and ex-

citement of the times never learned anything more about the case.

Several times during the course of the evening referred to at the White House, she observed a tall, handsome gentleman looking at her very intently, but, as she did not remember ever having seen him before, paid little attention to him.

As she was about to go to the cloak-room for her wraps, later in the evening, he approached her and asked, "Is this Miss R——?" She smilingly replied it was, "But I do not recognize you." He then asked her if she remembered Douglas Hospital, and her visit to the young man who was supposed to be dying under the circumstances above described. "Yes," she remembered. "Well, I was the patient," he said, "and I have never forgotten your kindness and the encouragement you gave me that day, and when I saw your face to-night, I felt that I must speak to you." Miss R—— was very much touched by being so pleasantly remembered, and after some conversation learned the gentleman was ex-Governor Connor of Maine.

Another very interesting meeting of the same nature, was that of Speaker Kiefer and the wife of Rev. F. D. Power, Chaplain of the House. When the

Speaker first met the lady in Washington, he was strongly impressed with the idea that he had met her elsewhere, but could not recollect where. She observed his puzzled air whenever they happened to be thrown together, but did not offer to relieve his embarrassment.

Finally, one day, he said to her, "Your face is so familiar, surely I have met you before this winter." She then asked him if he remembered the time he was severely wounded in Virginia and carried to the house of a gentleman near by for treatment, and of the little girl, his daughter, coming in every day to read to him while he remained there as an invalid.

"Yes," certainly he remembered. "And are you the little girl of that time?" he asked.

She informed him she was, and the Speaker was quite delighted to have an opportunity to thank her for her kindness, and let her know how much it had been appreciated.

XII.

CHURCHES.

THE religious belief of the incoming President is
always a subject of great interest to the con-
gregations of the different churches of Washington,
particularly to those of limited means and numbers;
for the church to which the President belongs, or is
in the habit of attending, is sure to be well filled
while he remains in office, and consequently much
curiosity is manifested upon the part of the several
denominations until the matter is settled.

It is very pleasant to have empty pews occupied
every Sabbath morning and evening by the hundreds of well-to-do people flocking in, also to have
an empty treasury replenished by their liberal donations. The new-comers do not often permanently
unite with the church, nor can they always be de-
pended upon to assist in its various works of benev-
olence; and the motive prompting many to come is

either curiosity or a vulgar desire to be associated
in the same congregation with the President, still
they lend their presence, are quiet and decorous in
taking part in the service, and very liberal in their
contributions, therefore are gladly welcomed.

It was the prospect of increased prosperity which
so much delighted the members of the Christian
Church in Washington when Mr. Garfield's election
was assured. They were sure of his presence with
them, for during the time he had served in Congress
he held a pew in the little frame building on Vermont Avenue, and was rarely absent from his seat
on Sabbath mornings.

They knew the tiny building would soon be entirely too small to serve their purpose, as it was impossible to seat more than four hundred persons,
and they immediately laid their plans to erect a
better and a more commodious house of worship.
Agents were sent out through the country to solicit
funds, and many large contributions were received
from persons in the city, and they bravely went to
work to secure a proper lot for the structure.

As is well known, the sad death of the President
was a great blow to their hopes and plans, but to
their credit it must be said, that although cast down,

they did not despair, but persevered in their purpose, and have now a handsome building on the site of the old one, which, when completed, will be quite an ornament to the city.

It was to the former little frame structure that Guiteau repaired one Sunday morning and watched the President through a window as he sat in his pew, and planned how he could send a bullet into his brain without injuring those seated near him.

Very many of the churches of the city have an interesting history, and the ups and downs, hopes and trials through which they have passed have been almost as momentous and varied as those attending the life of some individuals.

Upon some the weight of years is heavily resting, and the scars and lines upon their walls are visible signs of their long battle with Time and the elements. Others have thrown off the old form, renewed their youth, and have sprung up again in new forms of beauty. During the late war some formed a shelter for wounded and dying men, and the sacred walls which had resounded only with songs of praise and the words of the blessed gospel proclaiming "on earth peace, good-will toward men;" echoed back the wails of the suffering and groans of the dying.

Trinity Episcopal Church, at the corner of Third and "C" streets, was one of those taken for a hospital, and for ten months an armed sentinel paced back and forth before the door. A floor was laid upon supports just over the tops of the pews, and one hundred and fifty cots placed in it, all very soon occupied. On the 4th of July, 1862, fifty wounded men were brought in in the course of the day. Members of the congregation aided in administering to their wants, and the ladies were in the habit of spending much time there.

The church on "C" Street was not the original church of the parish, organized about the year 1826. The first meetings were held in the Circuit Court Room of the City Hall, and a house of worship was erected in 1829 on Fifth Street, between "D" and "E" streets. The building is still standing, and known at present as the Columbia Law Building. Reverend Henry Johns was the first rector, on a salary of $650 per annum—rather a small salary compared with that now paid some pastors of city churches. The present church was erected in 1851, and the location on Third Street selected, on account of being in the very heart of the wealthiest and most fashionable part of the city. The march of improvement has been so rapid that Trinity is now left very far " down town." Many prominent families of the city have been connected with this church, and Francis Scott Key, at the time of his death, was one of its most useful and active vestrymen.

Epiphany Episcopal Church, Fourth Presbyterian, and the Thirteenth Street Baptist Church were also used as hospitals.

The First Presbyterian is one of the venerable churches of the city. It was founded in 1809, and its first celebration of the Lord's Supper observed in the room of the Supreme Court of the United States. The first edifice was erected at the foot of Capitol Hill in 1812. In 1827 a new house was erected on Four-and-a-Half Street Northwest. This was soon found to be too small to accommodate the growing congregation, and in 1860 the present structure was erected. General Jackson was in the habit of attending service there while President. Mrs. Polk was a member of this church, and President and Mrs. Pierce were regular attendants. President Buchanan also attended there.

President Lincoln was a Presbyterian, and held a

pew in New York Avenue Church, of which, at that time, Dr. Gurley was pastor.

Christ Church, near the Navy Yard, is the oldest church in the city, but, like everything else American, has been subjected to the paint-brush, trowel, and chisel, so that all marks of age have been removed. The parish was organized in 1794, and the first church, a frame building, erected on New Jersey Avenue. In 1807 the present building on "G" Street Southeast was erected, and at that time was quite out in the country, and the congregation walked or rode over the commons to reach it. Mr. Madison was in the habit of attending service there.

The cemetery known as the Congressional Cemetery was originally the burying-ground of Christ Church. According to the original rules made on April 4, 1807, "no person of color," nor any one "known to deny a belief in the Christian religion," was allowed to be buried within the inclosure. There were one hundred burial sites set apart for Congressional use at first, and afterwards increased to three hundred. It is recorded in the church books, in 1817, that Commodore Tingey waited on President Monroe, and informed him he had been directed by the vestry to hand him a resolution passed by them, appropriating pew No. 1 in Christ Church for the use of himself and family. The President accepted the offer.

The Metropolitan Methodist Episcopal Church, so well known during President Grant's administration, is one of the largest and handsomest in the city. It is located at the corner of Four-and-a-Half and "C" streets, which was an unfortunate selection, as the ground is very low there, and the church set down in a hollow, as it were. It is of brown-stone, and finished with a graceful spire, the whole costing near $225,000.

The foundation was laid before the late war, but the church was not built for several years afterward. It was dedicated in 1869, and Dr. Newman became the pastor. He was Chaplain of the Senate about that time, and very soon gained a national reputation. Indeed, the church was in one sense a national church, for it was not erected to fill any special want in any particular circuit, and the committee solicited contributions from every part of the country. Several States and cities contributed liberally, and reserved one or more pews, to be designated by the name of that State or city. Thomas Kelso, Esq., of Baltimore, was very liberal in his contributions, and at one time gave $2000 to be appropriated to the purchase of two pews, one for the Chief Justice and the other for the President of the United States. General Grant occupied the latter, and was quite regular in his attendance upon the morning service. He was a trustee at that time, and I believe still holds the office. During his administration the church was packed morning and evening, and although it is capable of seating 1500 persons, sometimes many had to be turned away.

The spire was added two or three years after the church was dedicated, and with the chime of eleven bells, paid for through the individual efforts of the pastor's wife. Mr. Kelso was again the good friend, and contributed $5000 toward it, and it is known as the Kelso spire.

As an inducement to friends interested in the church to contribute to the chime of bells, it was agreed that any person giving $500 for that purpose, should be allowed the privilege of having their name inscribed upon one of the bells. Rarey, the famous horse tamer, complied with the terms, and one of the bells bears his name and the inscription, "In that day shall there be upon the bells of the horses, Holiness unto the Lord"—Zechariah xiv. 20.

The interior of the church is very handsome and made very interesting by the beautiful memorial windows, of which there are a score and more. They were contributed by the friends of certain pious and distinguished Methodists.

The keystone of the arch over the pulpit is a piece of Solomon's Temple, (?) and sent for that purpose by the United States Consul at Jerusalem. He also sent the cedar of Lebanon from which the cross upon the pulpit is made.

The elegant silver communion service was presented by a wealthy lady of New York, and Harper & Brothers donated the Bible.

Foundry Methodist Episcopal Church at the corner of Fourteenth and "G" streets has a very interesting history. During the war of 1812 there was an Englishman living in Georgetown by the name of Henry Foxall. He was the owner of a large foundry, and working day and night engaged in casting cannon for the use of the American army. The British officers had heard of the foundry, and were very anxious to gain possession in order to destroy it. After the battle of Bladensburg and the defeat of the American forces, the enemy pressed on to Washington, burned the Capitol, White House, and other public buildings, and were about to start over the creek to Georgetown to destroy this foundry. Their fleet was anchored in the Chesapeake Bay, and some of their vessels had ascended the Patuxent River. It was in the month of August and the weather very warm, and there arose a terrific storm which made the British apprehensive of being cut off from retreat by reason of their vessels being driven out to sea. So instead of going to Georgetown, they retraced their steps and embarked upon their ships.

Mr. Foxall was a Christian man and a good Methodist, and he attributed the preservation of his foundry to Divine interposition. and as a thank-offering for the favor vouchsafed him, erected a church where the present building stands, and named it "Foundry Church." He bore the whole expense of the building, and it was dedicated in September, 1815. It was enlarged in 1848, and in 1864 the present neat and substantial front added. President and Mrs. Hayes attended this church, and selected it because it was within walking distance of the White House.

The *Church of the Ascension,* at the corner of Massachusetts Avenue and Twelfth Street, for style of architecture, beauty of the stone, and prominence of situation, stands at the head of the churches in Washington. The present building is not the original one, nor is the site the same, for in throwing off the old form for the present attractive one, the congregation decided it would be better to move out of the business part of the city to a more populous neighborhood.

The original church was built about 1844 on "H" Street between Ninth and Tenth streets. The lot was a part of the property of Mrs. Van Ness, daughter of David Burns, the Scotch farmer before mentioned, who owned the land now occupied by the city of Washington. The family burying ground was there, and in 1829 Mr. and Mrs. Van Ness conveyed the lots to Rev. William Hawley and Arthur Middleton, trustees, who were directed to transfer and convey the premises to the vestry whenever "an Episcopal church and parsonage house shall be built thereon." The *Church of the Ascension* was "built thereon," and the Rev. L. I. Gilliss was the first rector. For many years the beautiful mausoleum, erected by Mr. Van Ness over the remains of his wife, stood under the shadow of its walls, and now stands in Oak Hill Cemetery.

The bustle of business each year approached

8

nearer and nearer, and the structure, never a very
substantial one, became dilapidated and in time un-
safe, and it was finally decided to move higher up in
the city and build a new church upon a more desirable site, still retaining the name and congregation of
the old one.   It was necessary to dispose of the old
lots, in order to pay for a new one, and here a question of law arose.   Had the congregation the right
to sell lots acquired as these were?   The matter
came before the courts, and after due discussion was
decided in favor of the church, and, with the assistance of Mr. Corcoran, who is a member of this congregation, the lot was purchased on Massachusetts
Avenue.   The present building was erected in 1874,
and the total cost amounted to nearly $200,000.   It is
of undressed white marble, with trimmings of cream-
colored free-stone.   The style is Gothic.   There is a
handsome tower finished with a symmetrical spire;
the windows are of richly stained glass.   The stone
glistens in the morning sunlight, and by moonlight
the pile is indescribably beautiful.   It stands upon
next to the highest point in the city, is higher than
Capitol Hill, and stands, as the rector once gracefully expressed it, "as a white-robed messenger from
heaven to earth."   "We have arrayed the herald

of peace in the vesture of peace, that it speak at once the glad tidings of salvation. Proclaim these truths, ye white and lustrous walls! Proclaim the Sun of righteousness while yonder sun doth climb the east, and when high noon he gains, and when he falls. Here in the nation's centre his beams will first salute on yonder Capitol the symbol of the nation's liberty, next he will bend his rosy steps to this pile, and salute with warm and glad embrace the symbol of that liberty wherewith Christ hath made you free."

St. Patrick's Roman Catholic Church is another that has thrown off the old form and sprung up anew in a new locality. The first church was on " F" Street just above Ninth, and erected about the year 1794. The lot was a part of the Van Ness property, and at that time quite out in the country. A few shanties were the only houses back of it, and beyond them fields of corn and grass. No street was open between the church and the Capitol, and about the only means of access to the latter was a road crossing a small stream in the vicinity of "E" Street between Seventh and Ninth streets. The first church was quite small and stood until 1810, when a better and more commodious building was erected.

It was of brick in the form of a Latin cross. Father Matthews became the pastor.

A few years ago this old church was torn down, and the site is now occupied by a row of fine stores. The congregation commenced a new house of worship on Tenth Street between " F" and " G."   It is of granite and gray sandstone in the Gothic style, and when completed will be one of the finest churches in Washington.

St. Matthews Church on "H" Street, at the corner of Fifteenth, is where the Catholic members of the Diplomatic Corps are in the habit of attending service.   It is not so very old, having been built in 1838–9. The music is usually very fine. The church is quite large, and has a projecting portico supported by six immense columns of red sandstone.

St. Augustine, another Roman Catholic Church, is quite new and remarkable only for having a colored congregation. The majority of the colored people throughout the South belong either to the Baptist or Methodist denomination, and it is unusual to find a flourishing Catholic, Episcopal, and Presbyterian congregation among them, as in Washington. St. Augustine has a very large attendance, and supports a fine choir, which attracts many from other churches to the afternoon service, white as well as colored. The pressure sometimes is so great, that an entrance fee of ten cents is charged in order to keep back the crowd.

President Arthur attends service at St. John's Episcopal Church on "H" Street. This church is very quaint in appearance, and bears the marks of age. It was erected about 1816, and is beautifully located upon Lafayette Park. It is built in the form of a Latin cross, with a portico supported by six large columns. The exterior is rough-cast or pebble-dashed, and would present a rather weather-beaten, unattractive appearance if it were not for the English ivy and Virginia creeper, which have stolen up the walls and transformed it into a bower of beauty. The interior has been modernized and embellished, and is now very bright and tasteful.

The church is quite small, entirely too small to accommodate the crowd attracted by the presence of the President, and there does not seem to be any way of enlarging it. The British Minister attends service there, also a number of officers of the Army and Navy.

XIII.

PARKS AND STREETS.

May, ——.

CAN any city be more beautiful than Washington this lovely spring morning?

I fancy not. One walks about the clean, smooth streets and through the public grounds delighted with the prospect; turn whichever way you may, visions of sylvan loveliness charm the eye and delight the heart; the parks are brilliant with crimson, white, pink, purple, and yellow blossoms; the velvety turf, sparkling fountains, bright sunshine, and songs of birds, make it seem almost a paradise.

The wise old fathers—who in face of so much opposition—selected the site for the Federal city and had it laid out upon so magnificent a scale, must have been endowed with prophetic vision, and one can scarcely repress the wish that they might be permitted to return for a brief period and look upon the present result of their wisdom and labor.

As beautiful as the city appears to-day though, upon comparing the original designs of the founders regarding its embellishment with what has actually been done in the way of improvement, we find the real does not begin to come up to the ideal in point of magnificence.

Some of the deviations from the original plan have been for the better; as, for instance, the site of the Washington Monument was intended originally to be ornamented with an equestrian statue of the Father of his Country. But how much more grand and imposing is the noble obelisk now towering heavenward than a statue of any kind.

On the high ground between the Capitol and the Anacostia, it was intended to erect an Historic Column, from which was to be calculated the distance to all places in the United States and on the Continent. This, however, has never been erected, and the ground is now occupied by the Liberty Statue, reared by the emancipated slaves of America. This is a fitting substitute, I think, for it marks an epoch in the country's history of great importance.

The statue, too, is extremely interesting. It is of bronze upon a granite base, and represents Lincoln standing by a monolith, holding in his right hand the proclamation of freedom; a slave with broken manacles is crouching at his feet, and the left hand extended over the prostrate form apparently bids it arise, stand up, and be a man. The base was given by Congress; the statue, costing $17,000, was paid for by the colored citizens. The first contribution for the purpose came from Charlotte Scott—a freed woman of Virginia—and were the first $5 earned in freedom.

The Naval Column, intended to celebrate the first rise of the Navy, and "to stand a ready monument to consecrate its progress and achievements," has not yet been erected. It was designed to have such a column stand near the river at the foot of Eighth Street West. As our navy has progressed backward instead of forward, there is little hope of ever having this ornament to the city.

Five grand fountains were to have been constructed in different parts of the city, and between the Capitol and the Botanical Garden a grand cascade, fed from the Tiber, was to send up its sparkling waters in forms of grace and beauty.

The grounds south of the President's House were intended to be laid out in walks and drives, and filled with flowers, arbors, and beautiful shrubbery. These last-mentioned embellishments have not yet been added, nor are they likely to be.

It has become a habit with moralists of the present time to dwell upon the simple taste and economical habits of our forefathers, and to hold them up as bright examples in matters of thrift and economy to the rising generation. No doubt they were more simple in their style of living than we of the present generation ; but I doubt if any one can read their discussions and decisions regarding the embellishment of the National Capital, without being impressed with the belief that their ideas of beauty and finish were both ostentatious and extravagant.

Although the original grand ideas have not been fully carried out, enough has been done to make Washington the most beautiful city in the country, if not in the world.

The plan of the city—the streets running at right angles, intersected by wide avenues, radiating from the Capitol—is peculiar, but has the effect of producing fine vistas, and of giving room for numerous parks and triangles; and as the latter are kept in beautiful order, the emerald turf in many instances enlivened by parterres of bright flowers, they form a succession of pleasant surprises, and alternate advantageously with the many equestrian and other statues with which the city is now enriched. Probably no other city of its size in the world has so many statues and monuments. There are, I believe, about thirty equestrian statues in the world, and Washington has six of them—one-fifth of the number of the whole world!

The Irish poet, who visited the city in 1804, did not have the same faith in regard to its future greatness and beauty as our fathers had, when he so wittily and sarcastically wrote :—

> " In fancy, now beneath the twilight gloom
> Come, let me lead thee o'er the second Rome,
> Where tribunes rule, where dusky Davi bow,
> And what was Goose Creek once is Tiber now ;
> This fam'd metropolis, where fancy sees
> Squares in morasses, obelisks in trees,
> Which travelling fools and gazetteers adorn
> With shrines unbuilt and heroes yet unborn."

The trouble with Mr. Moore was, he visited the embryo capital just eighty years too early.

"Squares in morasses!" Surely no man in his sober senses would think of calling the White House square "a morass!" The turf as smooth and beautiful as green velvet; the luxuriant shrubbery and noble forest trees, the beds of brilliant flowers, smooth gravelled walks, and sparkling fountains, are very far removed from a swamp.

Nor would he think of calling Lafayette Square, upon the opposite side of the street, "a morass." Seven acres of trees, shrubbery, flowers, and walks, to say nothing of the rampant statue of General Jackson, can hardly be called a morass.

"Obelisks in trees,"—continues Mr. Moore, alluding no doubt to the sturdy oaks and tall poplars so abundant in the city at the beginning of the century, —of course he could not know that Washington was to have an obelisk, to stand, when completed, several feet higher than any other structure in the world, to climb almost as high as the famous Tower of Babel, and to rival the Pyramids in solidity.

Nor could he anticipate such a thing as the sluggish waters of Goose Creek being so completely hidden and carried under an archway of masonry, and its surface turned into streets and roadways, as to baffle the attempt of the oldest inhabitant to locate its former course.

And the improvements and changes of the city would not surprise him any more than the political changes in the country; than in finding the shackles removed from the "dusky Davi," and instead of bondmen bowing down to the will of cruel taskmasters, standing to-day as citizens and equals, and more than this, holding positions of honor and responsibility, and having a vote and voice in the councils of the nation.

The city will be still more beautiful in the course of five or ten years, as the trees will have increased in growth and will make much more show than at present. There are about fifteen hundred varieties of trees and shrubs in the public parks and through the streets, including some fine specimens of the Cedar of Lebanon.

Why Washington should have remained for more than sixty years in such a crude, unfinished condition, and so indifferent to improvement, can only be satisfactorily explained by the fact that it rested during the time under the dark cloud of slavery.

Located upon a noble river, surrounded by a fertile country, blessed with a salubrious climate, the capital of a young and enthusiastic nation, with the national treasury to draw from, why did it not forty years ago become a leading city?

In little more than twenty years San Francisco grew from a mere village to a city of splendid proportions, and in wealth, influence, and importance gained more than Washington in seventy years.

Chicago, young enough to be the daughter of the " Federal City," has towered above it for years, and many of the villages in the new States of half a century now equal it in population.

Fortunately the incubus was removed, and since then wonderful changes have been wrought.

It required a terrible war to sweep away this blot upon our land, and Washington experienced many of the horrors attending it, but just as the fiery furnace is needed to set and increase the brilliancy of the tints used by the artist in decorating the delicate vase or rare plate, so was that furnace of affliction needed to develop, draw out, and make prominent the latent beauty of the Capital.

The growth of the city, strange to say, has not been in the direction expected by the founders. They did not have the acute perception of Bishop Berkeley in foreseeing it is "Westward the course of Empire takes its way," or their plan would have been very different. Instead of going eastward, as was hoped for, the growth has been in a direction entirely opposite, and instead of the Capitol facing the city it turns its back upon the broad avenues and public buildings, and smiles upon the straggling houses and unpaved streets of East Washington.

At present the tide of improvement seems to be turning in a northwesterly direction, and rows of palatial residences are springing up every year. Some of the houses are very elegant in finish and embrace every style of architecture. I presume no other city in the country can show such variety of styles.

There are specimens of ancient and modern architecture and of the middle ages. There are Grecian temples, Norman castles, ducal palaces, Gothic churches, and specimens of the Renaissance. The modern pile of brick and mortar, with huge, ugly windows, stand side by side with quaint and cosey dwellings of Queen Anne's time; and light and graceful French cottages are in pleasing contrast with handsome Italian villas.

XIV.

THE WHITE HOUSE.

THE White House is to me the most interesting thing in Washington, and I am glad the question recently before Congress—of building a new mansion for the President and retaining the old for an executive office—did not become a law.

There are so many pleasant associations connected with the building, such a halo of romance, as it were, about it which a new house cannot have, I hope it will be retained in the present form. No matter how imposing a new structure may be made, the elegance will not compensate for the loss of the delightful historical associations.

I never enter the wide, old-fashioned portal without thinking of the long line of distinguished men and fair women who have passed in and out: men, whose names and deeds are so indissolubly connected with the history of the country; women, whose beauty, grace, and intelligence have so largely influenced its advancement and culture.

Every nook and corner of the old place is interesting. Representatives of every civilized nation on the globe have been received there; fire, war, and the tempest have raged around; fashion has there held high carnival; intense suffering within the walls has excited the sympathy and tears of the nation; the spacious rooms have been the abode alternately of hope, sorrow, joy, happiness, pain, and ambition; youthful hearts have plighted their troth beneath the old roof, and the sacred mystery surrounding the entrance into life and the exit from it has hovered near. No single tongue or pen could begin to recite the story or the changes that have taken place in the estate belonging to this old family mansion. Spare the White House, Congress! for no matter how grand you may make a new mansion, a palace, if you will, it will not be the same charming old homestead!

Although the corner-stone was laid nearly one year before that of the Capitol, the mansion, as it now appears, was not completed until 1829. It was partially destroyed by the British in 1814, and restored in 1818; later the south portico was added, and in 1829 the north portico.

The style of the mansion is Doric, and is a modification of the residence of the Duke of Leinster, Dublin, and was suggested by Thomas Jefferson, to whom the country is largely indebted for this as well as many other things. His taste and suggestions were invaluable in planning and beautifying the National Capital.

December 30.

The old house is looking very fresh and attractive this morning in its new dress of pure white, and the open door so smilingly invited me to enter I could not resist the temptation to walk in, stroll around, and look upon the new adornments which have been completed in time for the usual New-Year's reception.

The vestibule with its mosaic floor of fine English tiles, frescoed walls, and roomy proportions, has always impressed me as being sufficiently spacious, and handsome enough for the purpose intended; but to-day I observe it has been greatly added to and beautified by an elegant screen of jewelled glass, which extends the whole length and separates the

9

vestibule from the central corridor. The colors are very rich and the play of light upon the irregular bits of glass very beautiful.

A courteous guide led the way to the grand old East Room, which would be handsome without any furniture at all, but much more beautiful with the present tasteful and elaborate adornments. The floor is covered with thick Axminster carpet of small figure in dark rich colors upon a pale yellow ground. The same dark colors predominate in the border. There are three large mirrors, and three immense crystal chandeliers.

The ceiling and walls are delicately frescoed, and a heavy cornice in white and gilt extends around the room. The furniture is of ebony, upholstered in old gold plush; the hangings of the windows and doors are of the same rich material. A portrait of Washington and of Lady Washington adorn the walls.

The Green Room, the next in order of the suite, is prettily furnished in Nile green satin. The walls are papered in the same delicate shade with sprays of gilt, and ornamented with a large mirror and a full-length portrait of Mrs. Hayes. A small ebony table stands before the picture, supporting the Hiawatha canoe, purchased at the Centennial Exhibition by Mrs. Grant, and used as a table ornament upon the occasion of a state dinner.

The Blue Room is now considered the gem of the suite, and may very properly be termed the Throne Room, for it is here the President stands to receive his guests upon all public occasions, and also the Diplomatic Corps, whenever the members may see proper to call. The predominating color is that known as robin's-egg blue. The floor is covered with Axminster carpet of antique blue-gray, the design a small oval figure. The furniture is of gilt upholstered in blue silk canvas, through which a golden thread is woven to give it a changeable appearance. The curtains are of the same material, trimmed at the bottom with plush of the same color, and at the top with heavy fringe; they are gracefully looped with folds of satin.

The centre of the room is occupied by a circular divan upholstered with the silken canvas. The walls are also of the robin's-egg blue, and are relieved by a frieze about eight feet in width; the decoration of this frieze is very elegant and very striking in effect. It consists of a number of geometrical designs, which being embossed upon paper have a raised look. The walls are quite dark at the floor, and gradually grow lighter higher up, and at the top are light gray; the lines are silvered and stand out from the surface.

The ceiling is ornamented with a number of silver ovals. The room is oval and the figures upon the ceiling bear an exact proportion to the shape of the room. Besides the central chandelier there are four sconces on the walls, each with seven gas jets, with pendants of iridescent glass. The background of each sconce is of glass mosaic work; the glass being cut into fantastic shapes and arranged in the form of a large rosette, with small mirrors inserted here and there. The effect is extremely beautiful when the gas-jets are lighted and the background flashes forth its rays from almost every point.

The open fireplace is surrounded with tiles of blue opal semi-transparent glass, and has a handsome fender and massive andirons.

It is only a step from the Blue Room into the Red Room—but how changed the scene! The floor of this room is covered with a thick carpet of dark red, the same small design prevailing as in the other rooms. The walls are of Pompeiian red, growing lighter near the ceiling. The latter is beautifully painted, and stars of bronze and copper glisten with great brightness over head. The walls are finished with a frieze, the design being somewhat suggestive of the stripes of the national flag. The windows are draped with crimson plush curtains, and a broad band of the same material forms the frame of the large mirror over the mantel. The most attractive thing about the room is the old-fashioned mantel-piece, copied from the style of the twelfth century. It is of carved red-wood, with panels of Japanese leather slightly sunken. Under the wooden shelf the space is filled in with glass mosaics, giving it the appearance of being studded with gems. Semi-transparent brown glass tiles surround the open fire-place, and the old-fashioned brass andirons rest upon earthenware tiles. A full-length portrait of President Arthur hangs upon the wall.

The State Dining-room is beyond the Red Room, but not open to the general visitor, only the privileged few being permitted to take a peep within. This is not much of a disappointment, though, for it is ordinarily a very plain apartment, and needs to make it attractive snowy damask, sparkling glass, glittering silver, elegant toilets, fair faces, fragrant flowers, and bright lights—the usual adjuncts of a state dinner.

A state dinner of the present time is a very different affair from that of the days of Washington, our first President.

At a dinner recently given by President Arthur there were thirty-six guests. The whole suite of parlors and the conservatory were thrown open and brilliantly lighted. Banks of choice cut flowers were heaped in all available places, and potted plants grouped about the rooms.

The ladies were in full evening dress, and the Marine Band discoursed sweet music throughout the feast. The dinner was of sixteen courses, and with it were served seven varieties of wine.

The table was covered with the finest and whitest of damask; a long mirror was laid down the centre, its edges wreathed with roses; an Indian canoe, about three feet long, composed of red and white carnations, was set upon it; the seats were represented by closely set white roses, and the body of the canoe filled in with Jacqueminot roses and leaves. At either end of the centre-piece were square cushions of moss set with calla lilies, and beyond them *epergnes* overflowing with Jacqueminot and Marshal

Neil roses. Flower-wreathed candelabras with waxen candles were grouped at the corners of the table. A choice bouquet, tied with rich satin ribbon, was presented to each lady.

The finest Presidential dinner given by Washington, in 1789, is thus described by one present:—

"The President, the Vice-President, the Foreign Ministers, the heads of departments of Government, the Speaker of the House, and the Senators from New Hampshire and the Senators from Georgia, being the two States from the northern and southern extremities of the Union, made the company at the table. It was the least showy dinner that I ever saw at the President's table, and the company was not large. The President made his whole dinner on a boiled leg of mutton. It was his usual practice to eat of but one dish. As there was no chaplain present, the President himself said a very short grace as he was sitting down.

"After the dinner and dessert were finished, one glass of wine was passed round the table, and no toast. The President arose, and all the company of course, and retired to the drawing-room, from which the guests departed as every one chose, without ceremony."

January 1, 1883.

This has been an eventful day at the White House. The customary New-Year's reception began under very happy auspices, but was abruptly ended by an extraordinary occurrence, made more remarkable by the highly dramatic surroundings.

The mansion was thrown open at an early hour and never appeared to better advantage. The parlors were in holiday attire, and the floral decorations profuse and beautiful. The city was bathed in a flood of sunshine, and under its inspiring influence both old and young entered heartily into the festivities of the day.

At eleven o'clock the President took his stand in the Blue Parlor, and was immediately surrounded with his Cabinet officers and the ladies he had invited to assist him in receiving the distinguished visitors who pay their respects to the Chief Magistrate upon the first day of the New Year.

The party formed a brilliant group under the central chandelier, and the exquisite toilets of the ladies were in keeping with the elegant surroundings.

Mrs. Frelinghuysen, wife of the Secretary of State, stood at the President's right, becomingly and richly attired in black satin, trimmed with Mechlin lace, worn over a court train of black velvet.

Mrs. Chandler, the wife of the Secretary of the Navy, wore an elegant dress of shrimp-pink satin combined with claret velvet, and elaborately trimmed with point lace.

Mrs. Keifer, wife of the Speaker of the House of Representatives, wore a handsome dress of Ottoman silk combined with brocaded silk in dark and light shades of electric blue.

Mrs. Senator Hawley was dressed in a combination suit of plush, silk, and velvet in shades of pale blue.

Mrs. Jones, of Nevada, was attired in pale pink moire, elaborately embroidered in crystal and garnished with rare lace.

The costumes of the other ladies present were equally as beautiful as those I have described, and the company an exceptionally brilliant one.

The President was smiling and gracious; the ladies all life and animation; the mansion radiant with bright flowers and sunshine; the new decorations and furniture invited attention; soft strains of music floated through the corridors and reached the ear of those waiting at the threshold to enter. A long line of officers and citizens formed in the grounds in order that each might enter in turn without confusion, and in the Red Room were gathered the Diplomatic Corps.

There were present the Chinese Minister in full Mandarin costume, wearing the red button and peacock feather of high State occasions; the Spanish Minister, resplendent in his court dress of blue and gold; Senor Felippe Lopes Netto, the Brazilian Minister, in his green court dress with its golden fleurs de lis, and upon his breast seven brilliant decorations; the Mexican Minister, Don Mattias Romero, accompanied by his wife, the latter wearing a gorgeous dress of royal purple velvet and a full parure of diamonds; representatives from Italy, Belgium, France, Turkey, and Russia, each wearing their particular insignia of rank. Would it be possible to find a more unusual or more brilliant pageant? and could anything be in greater contrast than the sad event which followed and suddenly ended the reception? The Honorable Elisha H. Allen, the Hawaiian Minister, wearing the broad badge of the order of Kamehameha III., led the way from the Red Room into the Blue Parlor, paid his respects to the President, chatted a short time with

the ladies, and passed on to the East Room, ex-
changing pleasant greetings with all the friends he
met.

Upon going to the ante-room for his hat and coat
he was suddenly seized with rheumatism of the heart,
fell senseless to the floor, and in a few moments expired.

Instead of smiles and congratulations, there were
awe-stricken faces and hushed tones! Instead of
music and laughter, consternation and hurried footsteps! Instead of eager, joyous anticipation, cold,
stern reality! Of what avail at that moment were
rank, money, friends? and in what respect did the
palace differ from the hovel?

The President, shocked by the sudden appearance
of the messenger of Death, ordered the house closed,
and that, which a few moments before promised to
be the most brilliant reception ever held at the White
House, suddenly ended in sadness and gloom.

XV.

THE LOUISE HOME.

IMPECUNIOUS old age always appeals very strongly to the sympathies of the humane and charitable, but when it is a refined, delicate woman left destitute, there seems to be a peculiar demand for help and sympathy. It is very hard for those who have spent the greater part of their lives in cheerful, luxurious homes, to be forced in old age, through loss of fortune, husband, or friends, to seek shelter in a public institution.

However well conducted such institutions may be, there must necessarily be many persons in them of uncultivated manners, and with habits so entirely different from one accustomed to the refinements of life, the very thought of being obliged to spend their declining years in such a place is repulsive to a refined person.

W. W. Corcoran was blessed with a lovely wife

and a fair daughter, and his conception of the idea of rearing an elegant home for aged ladies of destitute circumstances, shows his high estimation of woman, and its execution the most beautiful tribute he could have paid the memory of that wife and daughter.

Mrs. Corcoran was very beautiful, and died at an early age. Her daughter was equally handsome, and died a few years after marriage, leaving three little children. The mother and daughter each bore the name of Louise, and in their memory the husband and father erected the "Louise Home" for the benefit of reduced gentlewomen.

The building is quite imposing, and stands upon a high terrace surrounded with extensive grounds filled with flowers and ornamental shrubbery. It has been in operation since 1871, and was designed especially for ladies over fifty years of age who had never labored for their own support and were without money and friends.

Everything is provided for the inmates with the exception of clothing. Board, washing, medical attendance, medicines, and a comfortable room are furnished each lady, and she is not restricted in any way. Of course the places are eagerly sought for, and applications pour in by the dozen, but as only forty-five can be accommodated at one time, it is very difficult to secure one.

The building is of brick, with brown-stone trim-mings. The exterior is made very attractive in the summer season by a beautiful vine growing luxuri-antly over the walls. The interior is very bright and pleasant, and has been planned with a view to light and ventilation. There is a central rotunda of oval form open to the roof, with a glass canopy. The rooms are arranged upon three galleries, so that one is quite as desirable as another as far as light and ventilation are concerned. They are handsomely fur-nished with pretty Brussels carpets and walnut furni-ture, and the ladies add their own little ornaments and pictures.

The floors of the rotunda, galleries, hall, and stairs are heavily oiled, and the whole building heated by steam. The dining-room is spacious and well fur-nished; the glass, china, silver, and table-linen of the best quality and style.

With all this care for the ordinary comforts of life though, it would be dreary living if nothing were done for the gratification of the intellectual and æs-thetic taste.

I find this has also been remembered in establishing this attractive Home. A suite of handsomely furnished parlors affords room for recreation, where the ladies can enjoy music, reading, and conversation.

There is a library with well-filled book-cases, and the daily papers are laid upon the table every morning. Exquisitely beautiful portraits of Mrs. Corcoran and her daughter adorn the walls; there is also a very fine portrait of Mr. Corcoran, and various other works of art scattered through the rooms.

XVI.

THE application of book-learning to such a practical, common-sense business as tilling the soil, no doubt appears very absurd to the old farmer who is cultivating the ancestral estate to-day precisely as his father and grandfather did before him. And were he to visit Washington, would probably be so prejudiced, it would be impossible to induce him to go near the Department where they have a whole library bearing upon the subject.

Statistics about worms and bugs, rainfalls and frost areas, chemical analysis and kindred matters, are of little interest to him, and he will tell you, of no assistance whatever to a farmer, compared with early rising and hard work. The old man may, by dint of hard labor, manage to get along after a fashion, but the time is coming when his children and grandchildren will have to enter into competition with those who do practise book-farming, and unless they read up and avail themselves of the same helps, must be left far behind in the race.

We are pre-eminently an agricultural people, and it is remarkable, in view of the great interest taken in such pursuits by the founders of our Government, so many years should have elapsed before the establishment of a bureau devoted specially to the subject.

The Department of Agriculture was not established as a separate department until 1862. Congress had appropriated money for the distribution of cuttings and seeds some time previous to that year, but the work was done in the basement of the Patent Office.

The demands of the country gradually led to the enlargement of the bureau, and by Act of May 15, 1862, a department was authorized, the general design and duties of which "shall be to acquire and to diffuse among the people of the United States useful information on subjects connected with agriculture in the most general and comprehensive sense of that word, and to procure, propagate, and distribute among the people new and valuable seeds and plants."

A Commissioner was also authorized by the same

Act to be appointed by the President, with the advice and consent of the Senate, who was to acquire and to preserve in his Department all information concerning agriculture which he could obtain by means of books and correspondence, and by practical and scientific experiments; by the collection of statistics, and by any other appropriate means within his power.

The Department has been in successful operation ever since, and each year is enlarging the scope of its influence and throwing new light upon every question bearing upon the cultivation of the land, whether for purposes of food, clothing, or manufacture. The building, located upon reservation Number 2, between the Washington Monument and the Smithsonian Institution, is of brick, 170 feet long by 61 feet deep, with brown-stone trimmings, and finished with a Mansard roof. The grounds are handsomely laid out, and ornamented with flowers and shrubbery. The lawn in front is divided into an upper and lower garden, and in the summer season brilliant with parterres of bright colored flowers and borders of closely trimmed coleus.

The greenhouses, filled with tropical plants, are at

the west end of the building, and the experimental garden beyond them.

The interior of the building is handsomely finished in maple, walnut, and mahogany. The floors are inlaid in tiles of buff, blue, and brown, and the ceilings in some parts elaborately frescoed.

The library, on the main floor, contains nearly 13,000 volumes, comprising all the standard works upon chemistry, botany, entomology, and other subjects relating to agriculture. There are a number of foreign works, and a regular system of exchange is kept up with the horticultural, agricultural, and pomological societies of England, Germany, France, and Italy. These books are intended for reference only, and are not to be taken from the library.

On the second floor there is quite a large museum containing many interesting things. The plaster casts of fruits and vegetables are particularly attractive, and I think every farmer and fruit-grower in the land would do well to see them, and if he has any ambition whatever, he will not be satisfied until he can excel, or at least equal, them in his own garden or orchard.

There is a large collection of grains and cereals, both · native and foreign; specimens of flax and other fibrous products, stuffed birds and animals, and foreign woods.

Cotton is exhibited from the different States, and also placed in contrast with that grown in other countries.

There is a case filled with wool of various degrees of fineness. The Department has bestowed much attention upon this subject, and has spared neither time nor labor in making examinations and measurements of the fineness of the fibres. "It is difficult," says the Commissioner in a recent report, "by a written description, to make one unacquainted with the methods necessarily involved in the accurate execution of this work, comprehend the amount of tedious and patient labor required, but an approximate idea of it may be obtained from the fact that it has been necessary to make with the microscope at least seventy-five thousand individual measurements of fibres, the immediate results of which, to secure the accuracy desired, were of necessity relative, so that each one had to be reduced by calculation to the absolute standard. We have thus measured in all about six hundred samples of wool of different qualities, making altogether about 2100."

The museum is yet in its infancy, but interesting

exhibits are added each year. In the centre of the room is a large table 11 feet 7 inches by 6 feet 9 inches, made of a single plank of California redwood. It is highly polished, has a fine grain, and in color resembles dark mahogany. A large vase of Florida coquina shell-rock stands in the centre of the table.

The Department is very liberal in the distribution of seeds, and while a large share of the supply falls to members of Congress, to be distributed among their constituents, they do not have the exclusive use of them. Any person can make a request for seeds, and if it is within reasonable bounds, may be very sure of obtaining them.

From July 1, 1881, to June 30, 1882, 2,396,476 packages were distributed, embracing flower seeds, corn, wheat, oats, barley, rye, buckwheat, vegetable seeds, cotton, hemp, flax, jute, ramie, sorghum, coffee, and tea-seed.

The cultivation of tea in this country has not been a success, and the enterprise may be considered practically abandoned on the part of the Government. Individuals may continue it in the future for their own use, as experiments have shown that the plant will grow and reach some degree of perfection in certain Southern States, though it cannot be made profitable, and does not compare with the imported article in strength and flavor.

The pretty visions which for some time floated before the eyes of Congressmen of fragrant, steaming cups of Oriental tea raised at our own door, I fear are never to be realized. America is a great country and her people can do almost everything under the sun, but I think the manufacture of pekoe, oolong, souchong, and bohea a little too far beyond their reach.

True, we have the plant from which the above are all made, but we do not have the swarthy, almond-eyed Celestial, capable of living on a handful of rice a day and satisfied with a board for a bed at night, to manipulate it for us—to assort, dry, color, scent, and to roll each individual leaf into a particular shape, and to add the plumbago, turmeric, gum, gypsum, indigo, and other adulterations necessary. As a people we know something about adulterating; but we do not know exactly how much plumbago or indigo it takes to convert old hyson into young hyson, or pekoe into gunpowder, nor how many orange-blossoms, cape jessamine, etc., to add to give the requisite scent and flavor.

And even if we understood and could do all these things, I venture to assert the beverage prepared from the home-manufactured article would never taste just right to one who enjoys " the cups that cheer but not inebriate," for the reason it was not taken from a lead-lined chest, covered all over with pagodas, fans, grotesque figures in flowing robes standing upon the heads of others still more grotesque, and the whole having a peculiar, unmistakable odor of the sea. No! if we want genuine Oriental tea, we will be obliged to bring John Chinaman over to make it, and then will have to give each crop a short sea-voyage in order to have it just right.

Congress has appropriated $15,000 for the encouragement of tea-culture since July 1, 1880. Previous to that time 200 acres of land were leased near Summerville, S. C., and the work continued, with the help of the new appropriation, upon a larger scale than had heretofore been attempted. For nearly twenty years experiments have been made in a small way and numbers of tea-plants were annually distributed.

The climate of South Carolina is not the most favorable one for the growth of the plant, and the choice of land there apparently not a wise one, for

Mr. Saunders, the horticulturist of the Department, who was detailed by the Commissioner to make an examination of the plantation, reports: " With regard to the future prospects of the enterprise, if continued in the line of the present scheme and under the present system, it may be said that there is not much room for encouragement; . . however unfortunate it may be, it is clearly evident that the tea experiments must be made in a more southern latitude."

The Department has been rather more successful in the experiment of manufacturing sugar from sorghum. It has been demonstrated that sugar can be made from cane grown as far north as Washington, but whether it can ever be made a profitable branch of industry is still an open question.

The culture of silk is one of the most interesting subjects before the Department, and the Commissioner in his last report has collected a number of facts relating to culture and details, the experience of persons in different parts of the country who have ventured upon the rearing of silk-worms.

In view of the terrible ravages of grasshoppers, army worms, and other insects in various parts of the country, too much attention cannot be given to the study of their habits. The Department has entered largely upon this work, and a number of accomplished scientific gentlemen are at present engaged in making special investigations looking to the control of a few of the worst of our insect pests.

XVII.

THE building on the square west of the White House stands second to the Capitol in point of size, elegance, and cost. It takes up the entire square, and is entirely different from the other public buildings. The structure was commenced in 1871, for the use of the State, War, and Navy Departments, and is all completed with the exception of one wing. The basement story is of Maine granite, the superstructure of Virginia granite, and the stone has been finished in the most artistic manner. Notwithstanding the very elaborate ornamentation, the pile has a substantial and imposing appearance.

The four façades are similar. There is a projecting portico supported by groups of small graceful columns, which rest upon a massive granite platform. High flights of granite steps ascend to the portico, and groups of columns are used in the decorations all the way to the roof. The whole is crowned with a Mansard roof. The cost is estimated at $5,000,000.

The interior is quite as elegant as the exterior. A wide corridor, paved in black and white marble, extends around each wing. The staircases are of granite, exquisitely dressed, and guarded by balusters of bronze. The offices are fitted up in the best style, and some are quite handsome.

The wing devoted to the use of the State Department faces the Potomac River, and a fine view can be obtained from the upper windows.

The library on the third floor is a beautiful room, and prepared expressly for the reception of books. There are four tiers of alcoves, and the room is open to the roof with a skylight of ground glass. The painted parts are delicately tinted and gilded. The floor is of fine tiles laid in designs of various kinds, embracing circles, ovals, flowers and leaves of blue white, and brown.

The collection of books is very valuable, and there are at present a number of interesting historical documents and relics. In a glass case near the door is the magnificent silver vase, presented by the city of Philadelphia to Commodore Isaac Hull for his gallantry in bringing into action and destroying the

British sloop-of-war "Guerriere." It stands nearly
two and one-half feet high, is in the form of an urn
surmounted by a finely wrought silver eagle. His
sword and a pair of gold-mounted pistols are in the
same case.

In the centre of the room there is a larger case
filled with interesting objects, among them an auto-
graph letter of Peter the Great, an illustrated book
printed at Nuremberg in 1493, a club or sword-hilt
taken from pirates in the Straits of Madagascar, the
desk upon which the Declaration of Independence
was written, a whale's tooth, sent as a treaty by the
King of Fiji to the United States, Benjamin Franklin's staff, and many other things quite as interesting.

But the most valuable thing in the room, and the
most interesting to all Americans, is the Declaration
of Independence itself. The parchment upon which
it is written is very well preserved. A few names
have faded, but the text can be read very easily. It
is arranged in a sort of cabinet against the wall,
secured under plate glass. The doors protect it from
the light, and when they are opened it can be read
through the glass without handling. Directly under
the document is the original draft of the Declaration,
and to me more interesting than the instrument

itself, for it shows all the erasures, all the interlinea-
tions and changes made by the illustrious author as
new thoughts were suggested to him, or improvements suggested by those to whom it was submitted
for examination. It is only a torn, yellow, blotted
sheet of paper, but oh! how important in the results
flowing from the words inscribed thereon.

On the second floor is the Diplomatic Reception
Room, where the Secretary of State on Thursdays
receives the members of the Diplomatic Corps who
may be inclined to call. It is quite large, and longer
than wide. The floor is inlaid with hard wood
highly polished, and covered with two thick Turkish
rugs. Two long tables of ebonized wood with dark
velvet tops occupy the space down the centre of the
room. The furniture, consisting of sofas, arm-chairs,
and luxurious divans, is also of ebonized wood and
upholstered in figured brocade of sombre colors,
blended so harmoniously as to produce the general
effect of blue-gray; a gold thread is woven with the
brocade and adds very much to the richness of the
material. The three large windows are heavily
draped with the brocade, looped back with cord and
tassels over fine lace curtains. The ceiling is very
high and exquisitely frescoed in the same quiet

colors prevailing in the furniture. A large square mirror with frame of ebony is in the wall opposite the windows, and beautifully carved mantels of the same kind of wood occupy the space at the ends of the room. There are three highly polished chandeliers, and a pair of grates of burnished steel.

Portraits of Webster, Seward, Fish, Evarts, and Lord Ashburton adorn the walls.

Altogether the room is in perfect taste and harmony, and sufficiently handsome, I think, to bear the criticism—if they are disposed to criticize—of those who have been accustomed to the splendor and display of courts of royalty.

The ante-room contains a life-size portrait of the Bey of Tunis, sent by a special messenger to this country in 1865, together with a letter of condolence on the assassination of President Lincoln.

In the safe, in the office of the disbursing clerk, is kept the sword with which General Jackson fought the battle of New Orleans. The genial officer in charge relates with great glee the story of an enthusiastic Southern lady coming to the office one day, and upon the sword being shown her, reverently bending over and kissing and dropping a tear upon it, believing it to be the sword of General "Stonewall" Jackson!

The wing occupied by the Navy Department is very similar to the other parts of the building. The halls, stairways, balustrades, etc., are quite as handsome as the others, and the office of the Secretary a perfect gem in its way.

The library is much more elegant than that of the State Department, and the librarian claims that it has no equal in this country. The books are hidden away in adjoining alcoves, and the main room called the reception-room. It is thirty by forty feet, with an inlaid floor of the finest English tiling. The centre-piece is very elaborate, and represents a blazing star. The walls are formed of marble panels, those of the first story being of malachite, with narrow borders of Sienna marble and a wider border of red griotte from France. The whole panel is encased in a massive iron frame richly bronzed, and separated by pilasters with Corinthian capitals. The second story is open to the roof, and guarded with a handsome bronze balustrade, ornamented with mythological figures and inlaid with circular pieces of Mexican onyx. The gaslights in the first story are in the corners and supported by handsome bronze figures representing, respectively, "War and Peace," "Industry," "Goddess of Liberty," and the "Arts and Sciences." The chandelier in the upper story rests upon the prow of an Egyptian barge intended to represent Cleopatra's barge. On one side stands a female figure attired in the Egyptian costume and the other is wreathed with ferns and bulrushes.

The block of green marble over the entrance was taken from the temple at Pompeii. It has the word "Library" cut in deep letters and heavily gilded. The stone was presented by a gentleman residing in New York, very much interested in the Navy Department.

XVIII.

POST-OFFICE DEPARTMENT.

THE Post-Office Department is not considered particularly interesting by the residents of Washington, and strangers in the city rarely ever visit it. I had the curiosity one day to penetrate its mysterious recesses, to take a peep at the fountain-head from whence flow all those large streams and tiny rivulets, which find their way to every city, town, and hamlet of the States and Territories of our great country, and beyond it to every part of the world. I was both surprised and delighted with what I found there.

It is so very easy for one to snatch up a sheet of paper, scribble upon it a few lines, inclose it in an envelope, and address it to a friend away off in Oregon, or perhaps in Florida, or maybe in the northernmost corner of Maine, then walk to the nearest post-office or lamp-post and drop it in the box, feel-

11

ing sure that in due time it will reach its destination without any more trouble on his part.

All this has become so much a matter of course that one seldom cares to inquire why it is so easy, or desires to learn anything about the wonderful mechanism of this important arm of the body-politic.

The system has been brought so near perfection, and so many safeguards have been thrown around the mail-bag, that probably out of every one thousand letters mailed nine hundred and ninety-nine reach their destination whether they are properly super-scribed or not. The pains taken to deliver to the proper person every letter or package committed to the mail is remarkable, and no matter how soiled, how illiterate or apparently worthless either may appear, the same patient, diligent search is made to discover the person to whom it belongs.

A very good idea of the vast amount of work done by this Department may be obtained from the figures representing its disbursements and receipts for a single year.

For the year 1882 $40,482,021.23 were disbursed. The ordinary receipts amounted to $41,515,642.80, and the receipts from money orders to $360,767.35, leaving, after the settlement of certain outstanding liabilities, an excess of receipts over expenditures of $330,050.89.

These figures are also cheerful figures, for they show that, whereas in 1860 the deficiency was $10,000,000, it has not only been greatly reduced but an excess of receipts over expenditures of $330,050.89.

The amount of work done by the railway mail service in a single year will give some idea of what a letter-writing people we are.

During the year there were handled by the railway postal clerks 2,155,213,880 letters and postal cards, 1,278,176,630 pieces of other mail matter, being a total of 3,433,390,480 pieces, besides 14,234,310 registered packages, and 570,483 through registered pouches.

In handling this immense number of pieces, 902,489 errors were committed, or one error for every 3805 pieces handled. Considering that postal clerks perform their work on cars while in rapid motion, that they must work with great celerity, and yet make but one error in every 3805 pieces handled, it is believed that for accuracy this corps may safely challenge comparison with any other service in this country or elsewhere.

The Dead-Letter Office—so called—I found to be about the liveliest place I ever visited, and under the management of its efficient Superintendent is accomplishing wonders in the way of disposing of matters returned to it for treatment. I confess to much ignorance upon the subject of dead letters, previous to my visit, and imagined there was but one class of letters ever returned; but I discovered that there were at least six different classes.

A "dead letter" is one properly addressed, postage properly paid and reaches its destination in due time, remains in the post-office a reasonable time, advertised, and remains unclaimed one month. Of this class 3,049,952 were received at the Department during the year 1882.

"Hotel letters" are those sent by proprietors of hotels and boarding-houses which have accumulated upon their hands from time to time. Many persons go to watering-places and other resorts for a brief stay, have their letters addressed to the hotel at which they may be stopping and then suddenly change their plans and go off in another direction without leaving any address behind them. Of this class 83,189 were returned to the Dead-Letter Office during the year 1882.

A great many letter-writers in their hurry and carelessness do not take pains to ascertain if their letter is over weight, and attach one stamp when it may require two or three, and in consequence the letter is held at the local office for postage. Of this class 275,240 were returned to the Department last year.

Again, some articles are forbidden to be transported in the mails. Of these 954 parcels were returned to the Dead-Letter Office. 274,715 were returned on account of erroneous or illegible superscription, and, astounding as it may be, 11,711 bore no superscription whatever!

The number of parcels of merchandise, books, clothing, needlework, jewelry, etc., received during 1882, 60,476.

The total number of dead letters mailed abroad, 356,287. It is the rule of the Department to return these to their respective countries unopened; that is, to those countries entering into the Postal Union— and very few at present have not.

The majority of foreign letters returned to the Dead-Letter Office are for Italians. The representatives of that race in America are principally of the lower classes, and lead a migratory life. Hand-organs, monkeys, and penny shows do not pay very well if confined to one locality, hence they travel.

Emigrants branching out from New York and other seaboard cities, owing to their ignorance of the country and our way of doing things, are not aware they can leave orders to have their letters forwarded; and the correspondence following their arrival accumulates in those large offices and has to be returned to the Department. Again, country postmasters are not always able to read a foreign address, and not reading properly, unable to advertise the letter properly, and the party to whom it is addressed very likely never hears anything about it, and in time it finds its way to the Dead-Letter Office.

The statistics of the office are interesting as showing the contents of the letters. Of the domestic letters opened in 1882, 19,989 contained money amounting to $44,326.65 ; 24,575 contained drafts, checks, money-orders, etc., to the amount of $1,962,413.73. 52,463 contained postage stamps; 44,731 contained receipts, paid notes, and cancelled obligations of all sorts ; and 39,242 contained photographs. Sending photographs through the mail has become such a universal practice, and so many of them from careless preparation fail to reach their destination, it has been necessary for the Department to open registers, where a daily account is kept of the large number received. A description is given in the register, as far as possible, of each package and the date of mailing, so that the same may be traced and identified if application is made for it at some future time. Numbers have been returned in this way.

By reason of making the Post-Office Department a common carrier of merchandise, the work has been greatly increased, as well as the expenses, without commensurate remuneration.

People are so careless about wrapping, weighing, and addressing packages intended for the mail-bag, that large numbers of them in consequence find their way to the Dead-Letter Office; and as it is impossible to ascertain from whom they came and for whom intended, there is nothing left for the Department but to retain them.

There are also many unmailable articles dropped into the various offices over the country, and they too are retained. In this way many interesting and curious things have accumulated in the office, and it has been customary, heretofore, to have a sale of them once each year and the proceeds turned over to the United States Treasury.

During the present year the Superintendent has arranged a number of these articles in cases, and together they form a museum of remarkable interest. Unlike all other museums though, which have exhibits labelled and a history appended when it can be done, the contents of this one are without history. No one can tell from whom they came nor for whom the precious memento was intended, and one needs to make a personal inspection of them to be convinced that such things could really have been committed to the mail.

There is a fascinating mystery surrounding each article, and some of them so suggestive of thoughtful, loving care for an absent one, as to bring a tear to the eye of the interested observer.

In some instances, though very rare, the history is known, and there is a special reason for retaining them.

A human skull, for one thing, was sent to a physician; but as the postage was not prepaid he declined to receive it. Three snakes—a rattlesnake, an adder, and a spotted snake were sent to the museum in Germany—but as the mail is not intended for the transportation of *live* snakes in a perforated tin box they were stopped. They are preserved in the office in alcohol.

A sample brick was held for short postage. A large black leather valise for being above the prescribed size. A wooden wash-board for the same reason.

Some of the things are very curious! A petrified human ear may have an interesting history, if we could only learn it. A fossil fish, a box of butter-flies, and a box of South American beetles were probably intended for some enthusiastic naturalist.

An industrious and enterprising planter forwarded to his factor a miniature bale of cotton and a specimen of the same in the boll; but he will wait long for a favorable market, if he depends upon the factor's report upon said bale.

A bladder filled with snuff might have delighted the eyes of the intended recipient, but is rather an unsightly object in a museum.

From the number of spoons, ladles, saucepans, dust-pans, etc., some one must have undertaken to furnish a house by mail.

Everything necessary for a horse except a saddle are exhibited: bridles, whips, spurs, martingales, etc. I have no doubt if mail facilities are increased as much in the next twenty-five years as they have been in the last quarter of a century, we will be able to send not only saddles by mail but the horse also, and wagons and barrels of flour as well.

Pecks of ore pass through the mails. The museum has fine specimens of gold, silver, lead, and mica.

A box of tempting wedding cake is suggestive of a pleasant family gathering, with music and flowers and happy faces, and the disappointment of an absent one in not receiving some token of remembrance.

How irresistible is the desire to penetrate the mystery surrounding some of the articles!

One locket, about two or two and one-half inches square, containing miniatures of a lady and gentleman—from the style of dress and color of the gold in the setting must be at least a hundred years old—has been in the office *forty years!* What a precious heirloom it might be in some family to-day if the rightful owner could be found!

Another small oval locket, with the same style of setting, contains a very poor photograph of a young man in uniform. It was received in the Dead-Letter Office about the close of the war, and is supposed to have been found by some soldier upon a battle-field, or in a deserted house in the South, who removed the miniature, substituted his own picture, and sent it home to his mother or sweetheart. The back bears the inscription, "Mary Carter—Lucy Randolph—died 1783, aged 64."

There is a curious piece of German writing upon a large square of silk or linen cloth. It was given to a young man in the old country ninety-nine years ago as a certificate of good character and ability at the close of his apprenticeship to the grocery business!

Coins of all kinds, many of them very old and very rare, pass through the mails, and the collection in the museum is exceedingly interesting.

The Superintendent of the office has collected into an album a number of envelopes representing some of the curious, amusing, and erroneous addresses constantly received.

One bears the inscription: " if dose man don't kal for dose latter in ten daes, sand the bak too Miss _____."

Another was addressed: "the postmaster will please send this to my son who drives a yoke of red oxen, and the railroad runs through his place."

A third, the writer aspiring to be considered a wit, has the address in rhyme:—

> "Hallo! Uncle Sam, let me go in your mail,
> As I've taken a notion to ride on a rail
> To Illinois State, and there let me stop,
> And in McLean County just please let me drop
> In Le Roy post-office, there let me lay
> Until Reason R. G—— takes me away."

Postmaster's reply:—

> "Played out, my dear boy,
>   There is no use in talking;
> If you can't pay your way
>   You'll have to try walking."

A similar address to the above is:—

> "Now haste with this letter, as fast as you can,
> I've just paid your fare to good Uncle Sam.
> The case is quite urgent, so don't stop to think;
> Don't tarry for lunches, or even a drink.
> Lyman Street you will very soon find,
> Where the people are honest, good-natured, and kind.
> Frank T——, the man to whom you must go,
> Is at 46 Lyman Street, Cleveland, Hio.

It is surprising how expert the clerks become in detecting the errors and in discovering the meaning of many of the ambiguous addresses: A letter addressed to "Mr. Charles Gray, Bered Station, Cleveland, Chicargo, United States America," was delivered at Berea, Cuyahoga County, Ohio. One addressed to "Mr. William Hawkins, Buthemby, Penna.," was delivered at Perth Amboy, N. J. One to "Miss Mary Miller, No. 122 Virginia Street, Island," was delivered at Wheeling, W. Va. One to " John riley, fairfeld, highway," was delivered at Fairfield, Iowa.

There are one hundred clerks employed in the Dead-Letter Office, of which number seventy-five are ladies. The latter are found to be peculiarly well fitted for this kind of work. They are more persevering and more painstaking than the male clerks. They will follow up the slightest clue as long as there is a ray of hope of success, and their womanly intuition is invaluable in determining what names and places are sometimes really meant.

The lady in charge of the foreign letters is a German and a highly accomplished linguist. The ladies engaged in registering photographs, drafts, etc., are located in bright, attractive rooms, handsomely furnished, and the floors covered with neat carpets of crimson and gray.

The Money-Order Division is also quite interesting, and becoming one of the most important branches of the Postal Service.

The number of offices conducting domestic operations for 1882 was 5491. The orders issued by the same aggregated in value $113,400,118.21. The orders paid and repaid aggregated $113,388,301.90. The fees received from the public amounted to $1,053,710.55.

The history of the system, from its inception in England forty-four years ago down to the present time, is remarkable. Previous to the year 1838 the business had been conducted as a private enterprise by three clerks in the post-office of London. During that year it became an official department under the Postmaster-General.

In 1840 the charge was fixed at 3*d.* for sums not exceeding £2, and 6*d.* for over £2 and not exceeding £5.

The present rates in England for inland money orders range from 1*d.* on sums under 10*s.* to 1*s.* for £10, which is the maximum amount for which an order will be issued.

The Postal Money-Order System was established in this country November 1, 1864, and the bureau commenced with six clerks.

Orders are issued for any sum not exceeding $50; larger sums may be transferred by two or more orders, but postmasters are instructed not to issue more than three in any one day to the same person. Security is obtained by omitting from the order the name of the payee.

In 1865, 74,277 money orders were issued; in 1882 there were 8,798,312. The clerical force has increased from six to one hundred and forty clerks, and the business is now so extensive that it has been necessary to provide a building outside of the Department for its accommodation.

The work of assorting, counting, and checking the orders which pour in from all parts of the country and from foreign countries is very laborious, and requires the greatest accuracy. The domestic orders are sorted, first by States, then towns, and afterwards arranged in numerical sequence. The postmasters are required to send a weekly statement of money transactions to the Department, and these are carefully checked off with the orders returned, and the statements if correct pasted in books made to receive them, and then filed away for future reference. The files are increasing at a very rapid rate, and it will soon be a serious question what to do with them.

The Post-Office building is of marble in the Corinthian style of architecture, and occupies the entire square between Seventh and Eighth, " E" and " F" streets.

In the centre is a court nearly two hundred feet in length. A carriage-way opens into the court for the convenience of receiving and despatching mails. The cost of the structure was $1,700,000.

XIX.

U. S. TREASURY.

THE Secretary of the Treasury is an important officer of the Government, and upon him depends in a great measure the successful working of the machinery which Congress sets in motion. He is obliged to look after the lubricating oil, see that a proper supply is manufactured, that none is wasted or stolen, that it is properly applied where needed, and in times of great stress, when the supply becomes low, provide a way for procuring it elsewhere.

All this requires a master mind and the aid of many assistants, and as the country continues to grow the business of the Treasury Department increases in proportion.

The contrast between the working force of fifty years ago and that of the present is quite as great as the contrast between the old building of that time and the immense structure of to-day. The north,

12

south, and west wings had not then been built nor were they fully completed until the year 1863. The building now occupies a whole square, with two court-yards and a centre wing fifty-seven feet wide. It is of granite and has four fronts. The east front has a colonnade after the style of the Minerva Pallas at Athens, three hundred feet long with thirty large Ionic columns. The west has a central portico supported by eight monolithic pillars. The north and south fronts are similar.

The interior is finished in a very substantial manner, and in some parts elaborately decorated.

Fifty years ago the bureaus of the Department were only twelve in number, viz: the office of the Secretary, offices of First and Second Comptroller, Treasurer, Register, Solicitor, and of the six Auditors. Besides the Secretary, the employés of the Secretary's office were only sixteen clerks, with a chief clerk and one messenger. Now the business has increased so much it has been found necessary to divide it into nine divisions; each division with a chief and one assistant chief, and the employés altogether numbering several hundred. The Secretary is also assisted by two assistant secretaries; the duty of signing official letters alone being too much for one person's attention.

Besides these nine regular divisions there are several other offices, the business of which is closely connected with the Secretary's office. These are the Mint Bureau, Life-saving Service, Lighthouse Board, offices of the Commissioner of Customs, Comptroller of the Currency, Supervising Surgeon-General, Supervising Architect, Commissioner of Internal Revenue, Bureau of Statistics, and the Bureau of Engraving and Printing.

The Treasurer's office, fifty years ago, had about nine clerks, with a chief clerk and one messenger. It is only necessary to take a walk through the rooms occupied by that office now, and see the busy hands and heads at work, and the vast sums of money passing through the several processes of being counted, issued, destroyed, and reissued; to be convinced of the extraordinary growth of the office.

The Treasurer is assisted by an assistant treasurer, a cashier, an assistant cashier, and fully 250 employés, including chiefs of divisions, clerks, messengers, and laborers. The amount of work devolving upon this office is simply immense, and there is no chance for any drones in the hive.

The Auditor's offices have all largely increased, but more particularly those of the Second and Sixth Auditor. The late war increased the work of the Second Auditor's office very much, and business has accumulated so rapidly, although employing a large force, that they are still several years behind.

Fifty years ago it was considered quite an honor to be a government clerk, and many rose from such positions to fill places of great responsibility. Things have changed somewhat in this respect, and if a man takes a place in a government office nowadays, it is generally understood that outside openings have failed him, and he makes a virtue of necessity.

Women were not employed as clerks until after the year 1860, and the exigencies of the war period first opened the way. Twenty years of official life has proved their fitness for certain kinds of work, and at present there are several hundred women distributed through the various bureaus, engaged in copying, counting, and in some instances as accountants. For counting fractional currency and assorting coupons they are invaluable, for the male clerks usually consider this work as rather too trifling for their time and brains; and then, too, the women never steal anything. I have heard some of the officers say they would rather have them for this reason. They are generally too timid to try it; or, if tempted, take such small sums there is no trouble about making it right again. None of them have ventured upon $47,000 at once, as a male clerk did a few years ago.

Some of the female clerks become very expert in detecting counterfeits, and can single out a false note instantly from a large pile of genuine notes. They are also very useful in assorting, mending, and restoring mutilated notes returned for redemption. No one, unless he has made a personal examination of the money returned to the Department for this purpose, can form any idea of its condition. Some has been partially burned, some ground into pulp by passing through the wash-tub in pockets of pantaloons and other garments; some has been gnawed by rats and mice, and some so soiled and greasy one shrinks from touching it. It is a rule of the Department to redeem every note that can by any possible means be identified, and there is considerable ciphering to be done on some.

The Cash room is about the only really handsome room in the building. The walls are entirely of marble, several varieties being used in the construction. A balcony, guarded by a handsome bronze balustrade, separates the upper and lower story. The panels of the lower are of Sienna marble with borders of variegated Tennessee marble, pilasters and beads of white-veined native marble. Those of the upper story of Sarrangolum marble from the Pyrenees, with pilasters of white-veined Italian marble.

The hall near the Secretary's private office is lined with portraits of the former Secretaries who have departed this life; it being contrary to law to hang the picture of any one living there. These portraits form an interesting study, from the handsome face of Alexander Hamilton, the first and probably the ablest Secretary, down to S. P. Chase, the great war Secretary.

The office of the Chief of the Secret Service Division, located on the third floor, contains many interesting things, collected from year to year by the agents of the Government employed in detecting and breaking up counterfeiting.

There are several large albums filled with photographs of persons engaged in the business, and one is astonished to find so many of them of respectable appearance and apparently far above such contemptible employment. In the majority of them, though, "criminal" is stamped upon the face. There are a number of women among them, and it sometimes happens a whole family is engaged in making and passing spurious money. The men make and the women pass it. The history of one woman, whose picture is in the album, is remarkable. She has served a term in prison, her first husband died in prison, her father was a criminal, her son-in-law is serving fifteen years in prison, and her present husband is now in the penitentiary.

There are some curious specimens of altered notes in the collection; one, a twenty-dollar note, so artistically executed with pen and ink few persons except experts can detect the difference between the counterfeit and the genuine. It is the work of a consummate artist, and first passed at New Orleans. There is also an unfinished ten-dollar note, captured in Buffalo in 1874, the work of the notorious Ballard family. One member of that family offered to show the Government a process of making money which it would be impossible to counterfeit, and was willing to remain in jail while being tested, even if it required years; but the Government declined, as it could have no dealings with criminals.

Many artifices are resorted to for concealing the

false money. One of the most common is the cane device, and there are some curious specimens in the office captured at various times from counterfeiters.

Those persons who claim it is impossible to Americanize John Chinaman will be obliged to change their opinion after a look into the Rogue's Gallery. They are not only expert counterfeiters but the most adroit passers of the spurious money.

There is a picture of Governor Allen, of Ohio, hanging in the office, engraved by a counterfeiter while serving a term of years in the penitentiary at Columbus, Ohio.

Besides specimens of spurious money, the Department has a large album filled with specimens of all the notes and bonds issued by the Southern Confederacy.

Upon descending from the Secret Service office to the basement, one finds a neat, bright little room, where he can learn more about money, but it is genuine money, and being destroyed in such large quantities, would break the heart of a counterfeiter if he were present.

Before making a new issue of notes to a national bank, all of the former issue are destroyed, and great care is taken in counting and cancelling them. After they are properly cancelled, a committee of gentlemen see them taken to the macerating room, and there witness the process of unlocking the macerator, depositing the notes, and relocking the machine, to which each has a different key. The committee represent the Secretary of the Treasury, the Treasurer, and Comptroller of the Currency, and the ceremony is gone through with in order to prevent fraud or any suspicion of dishonesty in either office. Cold water is turned in upon the notes by means of a pipe and the mass is left to soften for several hours. The engine is then started, which works a double row of very keen knives, so sharp and closely set that a sheet of paper might be split in passing, and in about an hour the notes are reduced to pulp. The pulp is then drawn off, but in order to make sure that no large pieces have escaped, it is passed through a double wire basket, and the large pieces, if there are any, are again returned to the macerator for further manipulation. It is now placed in large tanks and allowed to drain, and then taken to the Bureau of Engraving and Printing and used in manufacturing coarse wrapping paper. These notes, as before mentioned, are from the national banks, and the money not always old and imperfect. When

a bank stops business, to enable it to recover the
bonds deposited with the Treasurer, it must bring
enough currency to cover the amount, and sometimes the money is perfectly new. The whole
process occupies but a few hours, and is a great
improvement upon the old method of burning, which
was not only extremely offensive to those engaged
but positively dangerous. With all the precautions
used it was impossible to prevent large pieces of
notes escaping, and during the process a fine yellow dust formed which penetrated to every crevice,
and was ruinous to papers, books, and furniture.
The present system is clean, effective, and interesting. From one to three millions of dollars are destroyed every week.

The business of many of the other offices is quite
interesting, but more particularly that of the Light-
House Board and Life-Saving Service. The latter
office has not only a number of models of the apparatus, guns, suits, etc., used in the perilous business
of saving shipwrecked men, but also numerous reports from crews actively engaged, which for thrilling interest can hardly be equalled.

Every one admires courage upon the battle-field,

and are ready to make heroes of those who in the midst of the smoke and excitement of battle perform some extraordinary deed of valor; but it seems to me the exploits of these surfmen are far more daring than those of the average soldier. It is a noble thing to save a human life, and the distinction increases in proportion to the risk and suffering incurred therefor.

Few persons realize, although they may have full knowledge of the facts, what these brave men really endure. It is a serious matter to be taken from a warm, comfortable bed at midnight to go out into the darkness and storm along a lonely, dangerous beach, to patrol for stranded and helpless vessels. For eight months of the year these patrols keep watch upon the ocean beaches from sunset to dawn, relieving each other at stated intervals, and march and countermarch to and fro, with eyes straining the offing for ships in peril. The way is long, dreary, and perilous. Often the surf shoots seething across the path, or the sentinel wades knee-deep, and even hip-deep across inlets which traverse the beach into the bays beyond. In the midst of cutting sleet, blinding flights of sand and spray, or the roaring hurricane, on he goes. There is a case on record of one man dying while making one of these heroic marches. But, it is when intent upon reaching a shipwrecked vessel that these men show the extraordinary courage and endurance which make heroes of them. Their efforts are almost superhuman, and more than one brave fellow has gone down in endeavoring to save the life of a fellow man. I am very sure no one could read the account of the wreck of the schooner "J. H. Hartzell," which occurred near Frankfort, Lake Michigan, on the 16th of October, 1880; or the disaster at Point aux Barques; or the wreck of the schooner "George Taulane," without having a higher appreciation of the Life-Saving Service than he ever had before.

The Treasury Department may be likened to an immense bee-hive. The hive itself cannot well be enlarged, for it already covers the entire square and stands five stories high, but the workers increase so rapidly it is necessary every few years to send out a swarm to establish itself elsewhere. One swarm moved out not long ago and took possession of a handsome new brick building near the river side, which was built expressly for, and much better adapted to the work of the Bureau of Engraving and Printing than the old quarters on the upper floor of the Treasury building. Here are made all the bank notes, bonds, stamps, etc., of the Government, and in large, jealously-guarded vaults are kept the steel-plates, dies, and other apparatus used in making them.

XX.

ALTHOUGH at this date (1883) the collection and arrangement of exhibits in the new National Museum are far from being complete, yet enough has been done to give one a very good idea of the general plan of the institution, and to show how interesting and valuable the collection must eventually become.

It will probably require several years to perfect the arrangement, but when completed there will be an innumerable series of object lessons, touching upon everything relating to man and to the globe he inhabits. The Museum will really be a vast kindergarten, where the smallest child and most ignorant man can understand and learn something from the lesson set before him. It will also be a field of incalculable value for the student and curious to glean from; and the tourist, who from choice or necessity, confines his travels to our own land, will there be able to learn all he cares to about other people and other lands.

The idea of the new Museum is said to have originated with Hon. Spencer F. Baird, the present Secretary of the Smithsonian Institution, and suggested by the Centennial Exhibition. The nucleus for the collection were the exhibits of many foreign countries, prepared expressly for the Exhibition, and at its close presented to the United States. Congress appropriated $250,000 for a building for the proper display of them, and they are being added to constantly.

The building is of brick laid in black mortar, with ornamental lines near the cornice of buff and blue brick. The trimmings are of granite. It covers 2.35 acres, or 102,200 square feet, and is of peculiar form. There is a central rotunda, octagonal in shape, with a dome, and four naves radiating from it, forming a Greek cross. There are four symmetrical exterior walls, and wide halls in the exterior angles of the cross, the whole forming a building nearly square. The roof, or roofs—for there are a series of them— are of iron. The main floors are covered with tile in fancy designs. The building is well lighted by numerous windows, in many of which are beautiful pictures photographed upon the glass, representing Indians, and scenes in the western Territories. In the rotunda is a deep basin with a fountain, constantly playing.

The heating, water, and gas pipes are conducted through subterranean ducts, and there is a perfect network of telegraph and telephone wires. There are no less than twenty-six telephones in the building, and electricity is made to do duty in many ways—lighting, moving clocks, burglar-alarms, call-bells, etc.

There are four grand divisions of subjects: The northeast corner of the building being devoted to American Ethnology, the northwest to the Industrial Arts, the southwest corner to Mineralogy and Economic Geology, and the southeast to Economic Natural History.

The department of minerals and building stones is particularly interesting, and those persons who have not given much attention to the subject are surprised to find such a variety of the latter and so much beauty in them. The specimens of marble are not confined to American marbles, but they seem to predominate, and one can scarcely decide which to admire the most—the pure white and the dove-colored marble from Vermont, the red, variegated from Tennessee, or the green-mottled from New York. Plain, perfectly black marble is somewhat rare, and I do not know if any has ever been found in this country. There is a beautiful specimen in the collection from New South Wales. The specimens of fossiliferous marbles in various stages of formation are exceedingly interesting, and in one of them—a dark-gray block from Lake Champlain— the veins take the exact form of a lobster, or some shell-fish very similar to it.

A specimen of semi-opaque marble from Virginia is interesting on account of its similarity to a slab taken from the lost quarry of Egypt. They are so much alike one would suppose they came from the same place. This Egyptian quarry was lost for over one hundred years, and rediscovered by a French-man in 1849.

American Ethnology has been an interesting study to our wise men for many years, and all new discoveries relating to, or throwing any light upon, the subject are received with delight. The various exploring expeditions sent out by the Government of late years have been very fortunate in their discoveries of pottery and other Indian relics, and their contributions to the Museum are extensive and valuable.

The ancient Indian is thought to have been a better artist than the modern, for the latter has been brought so near civilization, or rather civilization has advanced so close to him, it would be useless for him to expend much time and skill upon a frail earthen vessel, when for a few skins or a trifle he could purchase an iron or tin one far more serviceable.

The pottery now being arranged in the Museum has been found chiefly among the Pueblo Indians inhabiting Arizona and New Mexico.

The Moquis and Zunis are the most important of these tribes, and are semi-civilized Indians. They are supposed to be the tribes visited in 1540 by Coronado, who left many of the domestic animals among them. This is inferred from the fact of their useful vessels being ornamented with, or made in the form of fowls and animals unknown to the wild Indian. If they had never seen a pig how could they mould a water-jar in the exact form of one, and a spotted pig at that, with a curled tail?

In the collection there is a large bowl decorated

with the familiar form of a donkey (and the only specimen, as far as discovered, bearing this device).

Many of their water-jars are in the form of a duck, and, while the owl seems to have been the favorite design, chanticleer has not been neglected.

Some of their pitchers are of such symmetry and beauty a modern artist could not improve them.

There are tea-pots—or rather water-jars, for "the cups that cheer but not inebriate," were probably unknown to them—of the same shape and size of the Japanese tea-pots exposed for sale in any modern crockery store.

Some of the baskets are of graceful form, with curved handles and scalloped edges, and painted with beetles and flowers. Mrs. Stevenson, in her paper on "Zuni and the Zunians," says they are sacred baskets and intended to contain the meal used in their religious ceremonies.

Bowls, cups, canteens, toys, and dolls are ornamented in various ways. These articles are all unglazed, as Indian pottery is usually. Some of the vessels are perfectly black and highly polished. It is said, by those familiar with the subject, that this color is due to the burning and not to any coloring matter in the clay. The large water-jars of this black ware, with bulging sides and fluted necks, are really quite handsome.

The corrugated pottery is very curious and requires great care and skill in making. The clay is laid on in thread-like layers until the vessel assumes the shape desired. It is then smoothed and assimilated from the inside, leaving the rough edges intact upon the outside.

It has been held that the Indian is utterly devoid of humor. This may be true, or he may have it, and with his peculiar notions consider it unmanly to indulge in frivolity. I think, though, it is impossible for any one to look upon the grotesque form given to many of their useful and ornamental vessels without being impressed with the idea that there was considerable humor around, and when the deft fingers moulded the clay a smile must have wreathed the lips, which, like the loud guffaw of Artemus Ward while writing his humerous stories, was indicative of the spirit of fun within.

The dolls of the Moqui Indians are ridiculously grotesque. The faces are as stoical as all Indian faces, the stomachs very fat, and the hands, with digits extended, invariably represented as pressing upon them.

The collection of musical instruments of different times and nations is both curious and instructive, and shows very strikingly how universal the love of music—or what is intended for music.

Standing beside the modern cabinet organ with polished rosewood case, ivory keys, and perfect tone, one is inclined to pity or feel contempt for the people who can be satisfied with the uncouth ranat— exhibited in a case a few feet distant—and yet I have no doubt the Siamese think the music quite as sweet as the full rich tones of the organ are to us. The ranat resembles an infant's walnut coffin about as much as anything else, and has twenty-two strips of bamboo strung across the top. The music (?) is produced by tapping the bits of bamboo with two sticks.

Drums are shown in every variety and style, from that made of a hollowed log, used by the savage, to the perfect instrument used by a well-trained band. Guitars are shown in the same way, from the rude wooden affair covered with snake skin, to the pretty inlaid rosewood case and patent keys now in vogue.

The department devoted to the Industrial Arts is probably more pleasing than the others to a major-

ity of visitors, for the reason every one can understand at a glance what is intended to be shown by
each exhibit.

Scientific subjects require a certain amount of
education to be fully appreciated, and even then,
unless one is "well posted," rather dry and tiresome.
This department treats entirely of commonplace
subjects familiar to all. A number of useful articles
are exhibited, and the process of manufacture traced
from the raw material to the finished article. For
example : hempen rope is shown from the dried
plant with a few fibres separated, the same prepared
for twisting, to the perfect article—from the delicate
cord to the thick cable strong enough to, secure a
ship to her moorings.

Silk is followed from the cocoon to the handsome
brocade of brilliant hue and perfect finish. Gloves
are traced in the same way. First is shown the skin
in its original state, the same prepared and finished
for cutting, a glove partially cut from the whole
skin, one partly sewed, and finally the dainty affair
of fifteen buttons, all ready to grace the fair hand of
beauty.

Manufactures of fine horn are also shown.

Those who have been accustomed to think the Japanese only half civilized are usually surprised when they come to look upon the wonderful ingenuity, taste, and skill displayed in their various productions and works of art. By reason of the very friendly feeling existing between that nation and the United States, the latter has been the recipient of many beautiful and costly articles, which are all deposited in the Museum and are alone worth a trip to the Capital to see.

The Capron collection is valued at $15,000, and probably nothing like it in America.

General Horace Capron was formerly Commissioner of Agriculture, and in 1871 resigned that position to accept an appointment by the Japanese Government. He resided in Japan for five years, and rendered valuable service in settling and developing the island of Yesso—introducing new methods of farming, making surveys, introducing foreign grains, fruits, etc., and when he returned to Washington was laden with rich presents by the Emperor, many of them from his own private collection.

General Capron also improved his opportunity for purchasing rare and beautiful things, and together they form an exceedingly interesting collection.

There are seventeen pieces of fine gold lacquer from the Tycoon's private property, among them two beautiful cabinets, a large robe-case, a magnificent tray, at least three feet in length, decorated with open fans in rich gilt; a helmet case, chow-chow boxes, a sword stand, and an octagon stand for a bronze statue.

There are a number of large, beautiful screens, with paintings on silk illustrating the regulation dresses of the nobles under the old *régime;* also several with interesting street scenes, and others illustrating the holiday sports of old Japan.

The porcelains are very rare and beautiful. One pair of Satsuma vases, elephant trunk pattern, were made in the sixteenth century. Another pair of the same ware are very choice and of extraordinary decoration. The Cloisonée vases are the most valuable, and one rather small pair are of exquisite workmanship. The most striking thing in the collection is called a Silvereen, and was presented by the Tycoon to General Capron, and said to be one of the finest specimens of artistic workmanship ever sent out of Japan. There is first a pedestal or small table of graceful design, and of fine gold lacquer, the decorations and finish being very elaborate.

Upon this table rests a silver basket, from which ascend two branches of the Japanese plum tree, meeting overhead and forming an arch. The blossoms of the tree, and also of a flower entwined about it, are of silver, and in the branches a pair of nightingales, also wrought in silver. The combination is symbolical of friendship and esteem.

There is a smaller ornament of the same style. The pedestal is not so large nor so elaborate as the above, and instead of the silver basket a finely carved bronze represents a rock, and around the sharp points is entwined a trailing flower. A pair of birds wrought in silver are grouped upon it. These represent the national bird of Japan, and the beautiful plumage is exquisitely finished.

There are several pieces of wood-carving, and two specimens claimed to be over two hundred years old.

There are a number of fine bronzes, some of them very unique in design, and of great value.

The Museum also contains a number of showy Japanese robes and other interesting articles presented at the close of the Centennial Exhibition.

I think a case of wooden panels, showing the useful and ornamental trees of Japan, are about as ingenious and curious as anything they have sent us. The panels are of wood taken from the heart of the tree, smoothly planed and inserted in narrow frames made of the bark. At each corner of the frame is fastened a circular piece showing the grain of the wood. Upon the face of the panel is painted the leaf, blossom, and seed-vessel of the tree, thus showing at a glance the whole character of each tree treated.

The new Museum is not intended to supersede nor to interfere with the Smithsonian Institution. It is merely an annex of the latter, and the visitor or student will find, if he fails to visit both, he has lost much pleasure and valuable information.

XXI.

PATENT OFFICE.

THE Patent Office is decidedly the most pleasing—as far as the exterior is concerned—of the public buildings in Washington. Its vast proportions, classic style and substantial finish, never fail to command attention and appear equally well, whether viewed under the strong, bright light of the morning sun, or seen at night under the softer, paler light of the moon.

It occupies two squares, extending from Seventh to Ninth streets on one side, and from "F" to "G" streets on the other; is 453 feet long, 331 feet wide, and 75 feet high, and, up to the date of the last fire, including furniture, etc., cost $3,000,000. Repairing the damage done by that fire cost a quarter of a million more. This expenditure has been to a large extent out of the patent fund.

The building, constructed principally of marble, is

of the Doric style of architecture, and without ornamentation of any kind.

The east entrance is gained by a high flight of massive granite steps through a large projecting portico, supported by six immense fluted columns. The west side is finished with the same style of portico but lacks the high steps; the entrance being in the basement.

The main entrance upon "F" Street is remarkably grand and imposing. The portico is supported by sixteen large fluted columns, arranged in a double row and resting upon a massive substruction of masonry. This portico is modelled after the Parthenon at Athens and is of the same dimensions; from it a door opens into a roomy hall, with an arched ceiling resting upon large Doric columns. The floors of the corridors, which extend around the entire building, are beautifully paved in white marble.

The second floor is devoted to models, and has been constructed with a view to the proper exhibition of them.

Thousands and thousands of models are here gathered into glass cases, representing every useful and ornamental contrivance that the fertile mind of man can conceive. Some of them are apparently so simple and of so little consequence, one wonders why the inventor ever took the trouble to carry them to Washington.

Americans are peculiarly an inventive people, and as a people have reason to be proud of the system, which has been so successful in encouraging and protecting the genius for which they are distinguished. Foreign countries have not been slow in discovering the good points of the system, and are ready to avail themselves of the benefit of them in remodelling their own. Although the rules governing the issue of patents are much more strict in this country than in any other, yet America leads the world in the number issued. From an official gazette I learn that an approximation to the whole number of patents ever issued for mechanical inventions in civilized countries would give to the United States 200,000, Great Britain 100,000, France, 60,000, all other countries together 12,000.

Thomas Jefferson is said to have been the father of the first American patent system, which was founded under the Act of April 10, 1790. He took great pride in it, and gave personal consideration to every application made during the years between 1790 and 1793. It is related that the granting of a patent was held to be in these early times quite an event in the history of the State Department, where the clerical part of the work was performed. That when an application for one was made under the first Act Mr. Jefferson would summon Mr. Henry Knox, of Massachusetts, who was Secretary of War, and Mr. Edmund Randolph, of Virginia, who was Attorney-General, these officials being designated by the Act with the Secretary of State a tribunal to examine and grant patents; and that these distinguished officials would examine the applications critically, scrutinizing each point of the specification and claims carefully and rigorously. The result of this examination was that during the first year a majority of the applications failed to pass the ordeal, and only three patents were granted. The world moves! For Cabinet officers now to meet in solemn conclave to examine and pass upon applications for patents, would be considered something very remarkable and rather beneath their dignity.

In these early days every step in the matter was taken with the greatest care and caution, Mr. Jefferson seeking always to impress upon the minds of his officers and the public that the granting of a patent was a matter of no ordinary importance. In this, as in many other things, as the years roll on, does the wisdom, sagacity, and strong character of Mr. Jefferson loom up in broader, grander proportions. One cannot open a page of the history of the beginning of this nation without finding a trace of his hand upon it. He may, like many others, have had his eccentricities and weaknesses, but as a planner and leader was invaluable.

The history of the Patent Office shows that from 1790 to 1812 inventions were confined to agricultural and commercial objects. Implements for tilling the soil and machinery for navigation attracted most attention. The arts were poorly understood and little cultivated. The war of 1812, however, forced our people to attempt production in branches of industry heretofore almost wholly uncultivated, and the result was the most remarkable development of human ingenuity ever known in any age or country.

As is well known, the models and records of the office were entirely destroyed by the burning, in 1836, of the Post-Office building, where deposited. Everything perished, with the exception of one book from the library of little value to any one.

Among the many valuable things destroyed was a volume of drawings executed by Fulton, delineating the various parts of the machinery he employed in his little steamboat, and embracing three representations of it making its first triumphant struggle against the opposing current of the Hudson. The steamer was represented passing through the Highlands, and at two or three other interesting points on the river, with a beautiful sketch of the surrounding scenery smiling as it were at the victory which science and art had at last achieved over the power of the winds and the waters. This loss is irreparable.

The disastrous fire of September 24, 1877, was another great blow to the Patent Office business, and many valuable models were destroyed, but with the characteristic energy of Americans, the officials have succeeded in restoring the greater part of them; and the building, such a sad wreck upon the morning following that event, has been rebuilt, retouched, and refurnished, so that now scarcely a trace of the fire remains.

In 1837, the year following the first fire, there were 435 patents issued. In the year 1877, the date of the last fire, there were 10,416 issued. These figures show very clearly the wonderful growth of the business.

The halls containing the models are visited daily by people of every class, and those with an inventive turn of mind learn a great deal from the models exhibited. New inventions are often the direct result of an examination of some of them, in which another person, impelled by the same idea, has taken the first step, and so opened the way for final success.

The Secretary of the Interior has a handsome office on the main floor. The Land Office and the Indian Bureau are also in the building.

14

XXII.

•

UNCLE SAM has many big workshops in Washington, but the most gigantic one of all is found at the corner of "H" and North Capitol streets, known as the Government Printing Office.

The building—in the form of a rectangular quadrangle with a court in the centre—is four stories high, and exclusive of the stables, boilers, coal-house, etc., covers more than 41,000 square feet, and has floor space equal to $4\frac{1}{2}$ acres.

Just fancy $4\frac{1}{2}$ acres of machinery, type, paper, paste, ink, and oil, all being moved and manipulated for the transformation into books, papers, ledgers, official blanks, etc., by an army of active, intelligent employés, numbering 2200, more or less, and one can form some idea of this great workshop!

The machinery employed is all of the very best quality and most approved design, and the engine a perfect beauty. The employés, as a rule, are of a far higher grade of intelligence than those found in private establishments engaged in the same business.

Everything moves on like clock-work, and in the whole length of the building it is impossible to find a single idle man. The office hours are from 8 o'clock A. M. to 1 P. M., and from 2 to 5 P. M. Punctuality is required of every one, and a strict account kept of all time lost. Five minutes after the whistle blows means one hour lost time. The regular night force—for the office runs night and day when there is a press of work, and always when Congress is in session—go on duty at 10 P. M. and end at 7 A. M.

The employés are paid usually according to the amount of work done (by the piece), but some receive per diem wages, and some have stated monthly salaries. There are twenty proof readers, eleven copy holders, and four revisers. Some of the proof readers are versed in eight different languages—an accomplishment necessary on account of the books printed.

The proceedings of Congress, which were formerly published by contract with the old Globe Company, are now, as is well known, published in the daily

Record at the Government Printing Office, and this work is probably the most difficult of all for the Public Printer. To have a fresh, crisp, correct copy of the report of the doings of Congress of the day previous, ready to be laid on the desk of each member at the beginning of the morning session, is no small task, particularly when it is remembered how late the adjournment takes place some days, and how untranslatable are many of the written speeches. A wagon is kept running the entire night collecting copy, carrying messengers with proofs of speeches, etc. There are 6400 copies printed daily.

Seventy-two persons are employed upon the *Record* during a session of Congress, and nearly every part of the work is performed at night. The men work in a large room 60 by 90 feet, lighted with electric lights and equipped with new material and a first-class outfit in every respect. Almost every issue of the *Record* contains as much matter as any two of the New York dailies. The work is often very much retarded by the retention of speeches for revision; each member feels a little nervous about being correctly reported, and some awkward mistakes and strange mingling of politics might occur if great care were not taken, so that it is often after midnight before the copy is in the hands of the printer.

The amount of paper used in the establishment is wonderful. In the binding and printing office warehouses there are used about one hundred and fifty different kinds and sizes.

The report for a single quarter shows :—

Total ordered for quarter . . .	1,556,501 lbs.
Add map and plate paper ordered .	20,000 "

Most of the ledger paper for the bindery comes from New England. The paper used for ordinary purposes is made in Pennsylvania. Over 3200 tons are used yearly.

The disbursements of the office each year are nearly $3,000,000. Pay days—always an interesting time to the employés—are now the 3d, 8th, and 13th working days of each month. It is no small matter to pay such an army, and the cashier is often very much bothered before he gets through.

The money, which amounts to $50,000 or $60,000 for each pay day, is counted out in the cash-room of the Treasury Department in gold, silver, and banknotes, and given into the charge of the cashier, who locks the box carefully and places the key in his pocket. Four strong men then carry it out to the wagon of the Printing Office, and, with the cashier, jump in and are driven rapidly to their destination. The cashier never takes his eagle eye from the cash-box until it is safely landed in his office. The employés come in twenty-five at a time, in line just as their names appear on the pay-rolls. The name is called by a check clerk at the first window and the amount due. The cashier stands near a second window, counts out the money and passes it to his assistant, who checks the duplicate roll, sees that the amount is correct, and passes it over the counter to the employé, who is identified by the foreman or some assistant.

The pay-rolls amount to over $5000 per day, or about $650 per hour.

A large proportion of the employés are women, and they become very expert in doing certain kinds of work. On the third floor, where the folding is done, there are over 375. The pay for folding is two cents per hundred folds; when work is plenty they can average $25 per month. The woman in charge of the folding department goes around each day after the work is counted, verifies the count, and makes out a memorandum of the amount due. This slip is placed in a conspicuous place where all interested can see it, and remains one day for correction. It is then again verified, and placed on the book.

The office does all kinds of work for the executive departments. The millions of blank books used in Washington and all over the country for the various custom-houses, post-offices; the reports ordered by the several departments and ordered by Congress; Patent-Office reports, etc., are all printed there.

The President's annual message to Congress is also printed at the office, and in order to keep it from the public press the work has to be done in the most secret manner; but in spite of all their care the quick-witted reporters are sometimes too sharp for them and get the leading points, and then supply the deficiencies from their own fertile brains. The Public Printer was more successful with President Arthur's last message to Congress, and not one person saw it except those engaged in the preparation. After receiving the sheets from the President he went to his office, called his foreman of printing, chief clerk, and a few trusted employés, and each man took his "stick and rule" and "take," from the Public Printer down, and went to work. When the first proof was submitted to the President he was much gratified to find that the work had not only been properly guarded, but that his Public Printer and all his staff were practical printers, and could take good care of all confidential work at any hour of the day or night.

XXIII.

WORKS OF ART.

IN a city of large size with extensive public
grounds, one or two brass horses quietly standing upon granite pedestals, or, if preferred, rearing
in high-spirited style, are very desirable, and generally considered quite an acquisition. But there is
such a thing as overdoing the matter, and too many
worse than not having any at all. This is the case
in Washington. There is something irresistibly
comical, yet at the same time quite depressing, in
the brazen cavalcade constantly staring one in the
face. From one point—the corner of Rhode Island
Avenue and Sixteenth Street—there are three horse-
men in sight and almost within a stone's throw of
you, and these only one-half of the number the city
now contains. Two of them—Jackson and Thomas
—are bare-headed, the hat being held in the hand;
and when the winter's storm of snow and hail beats

down mercilessly upon the bared brow, or the scorching rays of a midsummer sun threaten imminent sunstroke, the passer-by is often possessed with a desire to replace it, or to hold an umbrella over the exposed head.

As works of art they are handsome and interesting, but entirely too numerous. One can form a very good idea of the display when they understand that six statues of the kind are crowded into the area of a triangle two and one-half miles in length, and about three-quarters wide.

This fancy for equestrian statues seems to have developed at the very beginning of our existence as a nation, and long before the Capital was permanently located; for the resolution to rear one in honor of Washington was passed as early as 1783. This was sixteen years before his death. The resolution was unanimous, ten States being present, and is interesting reading now, as it shows the high estimation in which he was held by his contemporaries, also how much ideas have changed respecting the style of these memorials of our distinguished men:

August 7, 1783, it was resolved, "That an equestrian statue of General Washington be erected at the place where the residence of Congress shall be established.

"That the statue be of bronze; the General to be represented in a Roman dress, holding a truncheon in his right hand, and his head encircled with a laurĕl wreath. The statue to be supported by a marble pedestal, on which are to be represented, in basso relievo, the following principal events of the war in which General Washington commanded in person, viz: the evacuation of Boston; the capture of the Hessians at Trenton; the battle of Princeton; the action of Monmouth, and the surrender of York. On the upper part of the front of the pedestal to be engraved as follows: The United States in Congress assembled, ordered this statue to be erected in the year of our Lord 1783 in honor of George Washington, the illustrious Commander-in-Chief of the armies of the United States of America during the war which vindicated and secured their liberty, sovereignty, and independence.

"That a statue conformable to the above plan be executed by the best artist in Europe, under the superintendence of the Minister of the United States at the Court of Versailles; and that money to defray the expense of the same be furnished from the treasury of the United States.

"That the Secretary of Congress transmit to the Minister of the United States at the Court of Versailles the best resemblance of General Washington that can be procured, for the purpose of having the above statue erected; together with the fittest description of the events which are to be the subject of the basso relievo."

This statue was never erected; whether opposed by the one intended to be honored, who, being a very modest, retiring man, did not care to see himself figuring before the public in such dress, is not known, but no such statue exists in Washington.

Nothing more seems to have been done in the matter until 1832, and not then until North Carolina and Massachusetts had each erected statues of Washington, and Congress decided it was high time for them to do something definite about one at the Capital, and in February, 1832, the House of Representatives adopted a resolution authorizing the President to employ Horatio Greenough, of Massachusetts, to execute in marble a full-length *pedestrian* statue of Washington to be placed in the centre of the Rotunda of the Capitol. The head was to be a copy of Houdon's Washington, and the accessories were to be left to the taste and judgment of the artist, and $5000 were appropriated for the purpose.

This, as is well known, is the famous colossal statue now standing in the east park of the Capitol, and the subject of more comment and ridicule than any other work of art in the city. It has quite an interesting and remarkable history, and has been moved and removed, and for a time was very much like a great white elephant upon the hands of Congress.

A brief description will interest those who have never seen the statue, and will enable them to better understand the point of the remarks upon the subject made in the House of Representatives in 1842.

The statue, without the pedestal, is ten feet high. The naked figure of Washington is represented sitting in a low chair, with one hand pointing heavenward and the other grasping a short Roman sword. A mantle covers the knees and is brought around and falls over the uplifted arm. The feet are shod with sandals. The back of the chair is elaborately carved and ornamented with acanthus leaves and garlands of flowers. On one side is standing a small figure of Columbus and on the other an Indian rests against the arm. On the right side of the chair is beautifully carved, in basso relievo, the figure of Phaeton in his car drawn by fleet steeds. On the left are represented North and South America as the infant Hercules strangling the serpent, and Iphiclus on the ground shrinking from the contest.

Across the back of the marble seat is the Latin inscription, "*Simulacrum istud ad magnum Libertatis exemplum nec sine ipsa dura turum. Horatius Greenough, Faciabat.*"

The resolution of Congress appropriated $5000, but the artist was unwilling to undertake the work for less than $20,000, which sum was granted, and he was to complete it in four years. The work was commenced in Florence, and instead of four years eight years passed away before ready for shipment; and here arose a serious question: How was it to be transported to the United States? After some discussion, Commodore Hull was ordered to go with a government vessel to Leghorn to receive it on board. When he arrived there the hatches were found to be too small to admit it to the hold, and as it would involve considerable expense to prepare the vessel for such a burden—the statue weighing twenty tons—he refused to undertake the transportation. A merchantman, the ship "Sea," after some delay, was chartered and her hatches enlarged, sides strengthened, and otherwise prepared to receive the statue.

The passage to this country was made in safety and the statue landed at the Navy Yard. It was a serious matter then to get it from this point into the Rotunda, and, although the distance from the Capitol is only one mile, it cost $5000 to place it there. The doors were found too small to admit it, and the masonry had to be cut away to allow it to enter. The weight was so great that there were serious doubts about the strength of the floor, and a pillar of masonry was erected below for additional support.

It was finally placed in position; but oh! what a disappointment! Nobody liked it, and the Committee would have been very glad to have returned it to the artist as not agreeing with the contract. Instead of a pedestrian statue it was a sitting statue, and instead of costing $20,000 reached nearly $45,000, for the artist sent an itemized bill, charging extra for everything except the design, and that was the very thing which failed to give satisfaction.

Among the items charged were :—

Cost of transportation from Carrara to Florence, 11 yoke of cattle, 15 men . . $262 50
Damage done to trees on the road from
Florence 60 00

Lease of studio for eight years, wages of foreman and assistant foreman, trough for working clay, servants' wages, postage, stone-cutters' work on the plinth and square part of chair, fuel consumed for five years, cotton cloth consumed in keeping the statue damp at night, salaries of the life models who stood for the statue, travelling expenses, etc. etc., in all amounting to $8000.

The statue remained in the Rotunda for one year, but very soon almost every one became convinced that the place was unsuitable for such a ponderous affair, and it grew at last to be a perfect eyesore to the members who were obliged to pass and repass every day. It was removed at last to the park and the doors again enlarged to take it out. There was no pedestal ready to receive it, and it was placed upon a platform of rough pine boards.

In May, 1842, a debate came up in the House of Representatives upon the subject of providing a pedestal for the statue which was provocative of some very sharp remarks and numerous witticisms.

Mr. Keim, of Pennsylvania, said that a suitable stone pedestal ought to be provided for it; he was not a member of the committee, but as far as they were concerned, "they were willing that the statue, with its wooden pedestal, should remain as it was, much like a Hindoo suttee, with a marble corpse on a funeral pile."

The statue possessed very high merit all, he believed, were agreed—conites or semi-conites, strict constructionists or latitudinarians, Whigs or Democrats; but he thought we had not taken that care of it which it deserved.

Mr. Henry A. Wise asked whether the pedestal was not, in strictness, a part of the statue; and whether Mr. Greenough was not bound to complete it for the compensation already allowed him.

Mr. J. Q. Adams was in favor of employing the artist to complete it, but thought he should be properly compensated.

Mr. Wise then began a speech and asked, " was it the wish of this Government that an *image*—a personification such as that—should be erected in the rotunda of the Capitol of the United States, or that such a statue of George Washington should be placed there ? He did not profess to be a man of exquisite taste and judgment in the fine arts; but, speaking as an American citizen, he must say, that that was not the conception of George Washington which had any place in his mind. He had been told by those who had far higher claims to speak on subjects like this, that to look upon that piece of sculpture made the blood to thrill in one's veins.   All he could say was, that it never had any such effect upon him; possibly because he had never looked long enough upon it at any one time.

"He must confess it had on him much the same effect as it had produced on a gentleman of Maryland, one of the olden time, a gentleman of the old school, who having heard so much said of this statue, mounted his horse and rode a long distance purposely to look at it.   Having hitched his horse before the Capitol he mounted the steps and entered the rotunda, where, after looking at the statue for a few seconds, turned from it as, he said, the father of his country would do, who was the most modest of men.

"What was it but a plagiarism from the heathen mythology to represent a Christian hero a Jupiter Tonans, or a Jupiter Stator, in place of an American hero and sage?—a naked statue of George Washington! of a man whose skin had probably never been looked upon by any living person.   It might possibly suit modern Italian taste, but certainly it did not the American."

After criticizing the Latin inscription Mr. Wise continued: "A countryman entering the rotunda by the Library door and seeing the back of the statue, would very naturally ask, Who is this? and looking at the inscription, would say to himself, Simul Acrum! Who is Simul Acrum? But the next word (istud) would tell him.

"It was offensive, he did not like the position of one hand, as if holding up the clouds—a position better suited to ' the cloud-compelling Jove'—and to the gracious surrender of his sword with the other, which some Irishman had mistaken for a harp."

He also sharply criticized the left " shin," and seemed no better pleased with the naked feet and sandals. He would like to cut off the head and throw the remainder into the Potomac, so as to hide it from all the world, like Persico wanted to do at Richmond when he saw Houdon's statue of Washington represented in a military dress.

The statue now stands upon a massive granite pedestal twelve feet high, and is much improved, but should be ten or fifteen feet higher to properly soften the heavy lines and hide the defects.

It must have been a bitter disappointment to the artist to find his work so little appreciated, and I have no doubt he anticipated the most flattering compliments and acknowledgments from Congress upon his wonderful success. That he fully appreciated it himself can be inferred from an extract from one of his letters to Daniel Webster, then Secretary of State. Writing from Florence in 1841 about the statue, he says: "It is the birth of my thought; I have sacrificed to it the flower of my days and the freshness of my strength; its every lineament has been moistened with the sweat of my toil and the tears of my exile. I would not barter away its associations with my name for the proudest fortune that avarice ever dreamed."

An order for an equestrian statue of Washington was given to Mr. Clark Mills in 1853, and the sum of $50,000 appropriated for the purpose. Mr. Mills had finished his statue of General Jackson the year before, which was begun under the auspices of the Jackson Monument Committee, but completed by Congress; and as the public were pleased with it, he succeeded in securing an order for the statue of General Washington. Congress voted cannon for the metal of both.

The erection of an equestrian statue at the national Capital in honor of General Nathaniel Greene, of

Rhode Island, was eminently appropriate, yet, after all, but a tardy act of justice. General Greene was one of the most dashing, brilliant officers of the Revolutionary period. He served from 1775 in actual service, without a day's furlough, till the final disbandment of the army in 1783, besides spending large sums of money in clothing and feeding the suffering soldiers.

August 8, 1786, Congress passed a resolution appropriating $500 for a monument to be erected to his memory at the seat of the Federal Government; but, somehow, the matter was overlooked and nothing more done about it until 1874, when Congress appropriated $40,000 for an equestrian statue in his honor. This was unveiled in 1878, ninety years having elapsed between the date of the original resolution and the completion of the work.

All trace of his burial place has been lost. The statue is of bronze and represents the General in the uniform of an officer of the Continental Army; his arm extended and pointing forward as though in the act of giving orders upon the field of battle.

The beautiful Naval Monument on Pennsylvania Avenue at the foot of Capitol Hill, and near the entrance to the grounds, is, to me, very much out of place. It is so completely overshadowed by the Capitol and the lofty dome that the beauty is almost entirely lost. Such a costly and artistic group as this should have been given an isolated, prominent position.

It was suggested and designed by Admiral Porter, and the subscription list, starting in his fleet in 1865, grew very rapidly, until $10,000 were collected. Congress appropriated $20,000 more, and several interested friends made large contributions. The monument was executed in Italy, and was erected "in memory of the officers, seamen, and marines of the United States Navy who fell in defence of the Union and Liberty of their country, 1861–65." It is of fine Carrara marble and about forty feet high. The surmounting figures represent America and ·History; the latter is recording the woes her suffering sister whispers into her ear. On the west side of the plinth Victory crowns young Neptune and Mars. On the east side Peace stands offering the olive branch, and at her feet are gathered the products of the peaceful arts.

The whole thing is very chaste and beautiful, and, moreover, a good illustration of our indebtedness to

the Greeks and Romans for their fanciful, mythological representations. There might have been grouped
upon it a uniformed officer, a rough sailor, and a
full-rigged ship; and coils of ropes, anchors, and
miniature guns might have been used for the minor
adornments, but how much more beautiful are the
graceful forms and flowing robes of the ideal females
representing Peace, America, History, and Victory.

The Indian formerly occupied a prominent place
in the statuary and paintings added to the Capitol,
and it has only been a short time since he was dis.
pensed with altogether. He was usually represented
in his native dress of paint and feathers, and about
to engage in some dreadful deed of blood.

On the blockings east of the Capitol are two semi-
colossal groups of statuary and an Indian figure in
each.

The smaller of the two is by Persico, and represents Columbus holding aloft a small globe, which
he is explaining to an Indian woman crouching at
his side. The work is very beautifully executed, and
the artist was engaged upon it five years. The cost
was $24,000. A wag once described it to a friend
as "Columbus playing ball with an Indian woman."

The other group, known as "The Rescue," is much

larger. Greenough, the artist, was twelve years in completing it, and received $30,000 for his work. There are five figures in the group—a dog, a woman with an infant in her arms, and a huge hunter wrestling with a naked Indian.

These groups have been in position about thirty years, and, from the exposure to our trying climate, are very much blackened and much of their beauty marred.

Mr. Greenough anticipated this effect and was extremely anxious to produce his design in bronze. He was in Florence at the time, and wrote on to Washington suggesting the use of the latter, giving his reasons for preferring it. In his letter he says, "I have lately exhibited to the public in this city the model of the group on which I am employed for the United States Government, and which is intended for one of the blockings which flank the stairs of the eastern front of the Capitol. The marble for the same is now in process of quarrying, and I shall hasten the work as far as is consistent with the demands of the art. I cannot, however, let slip this opportunity of raising my voice once more on the subject of the material to be employed in executing this group. Intended, as it is, to stand in the open air, exposed to a climate far more destructive than that of Florence, I cannot help but think that bronze were preferable to marble. The bronzes erected during the reign of Cosmo the First are as fresh and sharp at this day as when erected. The color they have assumed from exposure adds to their grandeur, and makes them not less venerable as monuments than beautiful as feats of art. The marbles erected during the same reign have lost that unity of color which is the first element of effect in statuary; they retain their original snowy whiteness in those parts not subject to be granulated by the rain and frost, while they are positively black in all the more prominent and exposed portions."

The use of bronze instead of marble for these groups would have greatly increased the cost, but the durability was worth considering. Thirty years from now they will probably be perfectly black.

Just above these groups, in the niches each side of the great bronze door, are two very beautiful statues by Persico. As they are sheltered by the projecting portico the climate has had no effect upon them.

One is a representation of Peace and the other of War, or, in other words, Ceres and Mars, and although the design is not original they are well executed, and considered fine specimens of art. The artist was engaged upon them five or six years, and received $24,000. They are of Carrara marble.

Some of the fountains in the city are quite artistic in design, and deserve a passing notice. The immense granite vase standing upon the tesselated pavement on the north side of the Treasury Department measures twelve feet across the top, and is cut from a single block of granite. The water rises in the centre of the bowl in the form of a small circle, fills it, and falls over the edge into a deep basin below, and although not thrown very high, the fountain is attractive on account of its novelty.

The drinking fountain on the west side of the Capitol is entirely too handsome to be hidden away, as it is, under the steps leading up to the Rotunda. It was designed by Powers, erected in 1836, and cost over one thousand dollars. There is a plinth of white marble about ten feet in height; at the corners are columns of polished blue-veined marble with white capitals. These support an entablature, and the whole is surmounted with an ornamental vase. The water flows from a bronze faucet into a large bronze vase, sunken in a broad marble platform. The platform is very much worn at the edges, and, if the hollows are indicative of the number of feet pressing upon it, tens of thousands must have quenched their thirst at the fountain in the last forty-five years. It stood, of course, through the late war, and I have no doubt the marks of rough usage it now bears were made during that period.

The Bartholdi Fountain, so conspicuous near the entrance of the Main Building at the Centennial Exbition and afterward purchased by the Government for $6000, now ornaments the Botanical Garden. It is quite imposing when playing, but at other times has very much the appearance of being placed there temporarily until a suitable place can be found to receive it, a sort of unfinished, unsettled look. There was some disappointment upon the part of the Government after the purchase. The fountain was supposed to be of bronze, but after exposure to the weather found to be of iron bronzed, and of course not worth the price paid.

The latest addition to the works of art in the city is the pedestrian statue of Professor Joseph Henry,

unveiled April 19, 1883. It is of bronze upon a
pedestal of Scotch granite, and stands upon the lawn
directly in front of the Smithsonian Institution, of
which for so many years the Professor was the honored Secretary.   W. W. Story was the artist.

XXIV.

CONGRESSIONAL CEMETERY.

ONE lovely evening in June I strolled out to the Congressional Cemetery, which is located upon the brow of a hill overlooking the Eastern Branch about one mile and a half from the Capitol.

The spot is a singularly attractive one, and on this particular evening appeared at its very best. The foliage and the roses were in perfection. The new-mown hay in the surrounding meadows filled the air with fragrance. The sluggish waters of the Branch flowed noiselessly around the curves of the sloping bank; the high hills on the Maryland side clothed in beautiful verdure formed a charming background to the pleasing picture, and no sound was heard to break the stillness save the songs of birds and the clear notes of a bugle from the Navy Yard near by, calling the men from their quarters for evening drill.

A truly lovely spot for that long, long sleep which

awaits each mortal, and also a beautiful calm retreat where the living may spend a quiet hour, away from the noise, bustle, and weariness of the city.

There are many distinguished persons buried in the Cemetery. In a prominent place stands the very imposing monument over the grave of William Wirt, Attorney-General from 1817 to 1829, and author of the "Life of Patrick Henry."

In the northeast portion is the high monument of Elbridge Gerry, one of the signers of the Declaration of Independence and the fifth Vice-President of the United States; and near it that of George Clinton, who was a member of the Continental Congress, voted for the Declaration of Independence, distinguished himself in the Revolutionary War, and was Vice-President with Thomas Jefferson as President.

Within a stone's throw of the graves of these distinguished patriots is the unmarked resting-place of Herold, one of the conspirators engaged in the assassination of President Lincoln, and the companion of Booth in his wild flight through Maryland after the dreadful deed.

In spite of my knowledge of his terrible crime, a feeling of pity filled my breast as I looked upon his grave beside those of the parents who gave him life, and thought of the mother whose heart was broken by the awful end of her much-loved boy.

His parents are said to have been very respectable people, and his father at one time held quite a responsible position under the Government. This boy —for he was only about twenty-two—never gave any evidence of great intellectual force, and evil companions and strong drink probably had more to do with his unhappy career than a really depraved nature.

In the same part of the Cemetery is the grave of Push Ma-ta-ha, a Choctaw Chief, who died in Washington in 1824 while on a visit to the Great White Father. He was a renowned chief in the councils of his nation, and always the white man's friend. His association with the white man made him ambitious of earthly honors, for almost his last words were: "When I am gone let the big guns be fired over me!" His brother chiefs erected a monument over him, and these words are a part of the inscription.

Near the brow of the hill is the very handsome monument of General Alexander Macomb, at one time Commander-in-Chief of the United States Army; also the broken column erected in honor of Major-General Jacob Brown. A number of the old residents of the city are buried in the cemetery, and some of the graves date back to the beginning of the century.

One peculiar feature of the place is the small stone cenotaphs erected in memory of deceased Congressmen. There are two long rows, and, strange to say, only five or six of those whose names appear upon them are buried there. It was formerly considered an honor to have such a monument erected, but the custom has been done away with, and it is only in cases of actual burial that such stones are now erected.

The Cemetery was originally the burying ground of Christ Church, and in return for donations of land and money one hundred burial-sites were set apart for the use of Congress. The number was afterward increased to three hundred.

XXV.

WASHINGTON MONUMENT.

THE beautiful Capitol, with its lofty dome, will have to share honors very soon with the Washington Monument, now approaching completion; for if the original plan is adhered to, the latter will tower above it nearly two hundred feet. It is now about thirty feet higher than the Goddess of Liberty upon the dome.

It is to be regretted that a structure as massive and costly as this obelisk should not have been made more beautiful. It is conspicuous for the absence of beauty, and the one idea of the originators seems to have been a determination to build a shaft higher than anything else in the world; a genuine American idea to "beat all creation" without regard to cost or effect.

True, the original design embraced additions very grand and magnificent in themselves, but not at all

16

in keeping with our way of building, living, and doing things generally, and it was found almost at the start that it would have to be very much modified.

It was intended to have a grand circular colonnaded building 250 feet in diameter, and 100 feet high, from which was to spring an obelisk shaft 70 feet at base and 500 feet high.

The vast rotunda forming the grand base of the monument is surrounded by 30 columns of massive proportions, being 12 feet in diameter and 45 feet high, elevated upon a lofty base or stylobate of 20 feet elevation and 300 feet square, surmounted by an entablature 20 feet high, and crowned by a massive balustrade 15 feet high.

A tetrastyle portico (4 columns in front) in triple rows of the same proportions and order with the columns of the colonnade, distinguishes the entrance to the monument and serves as a pedestal for the triumphal car and statue of the illustrious Chief; the steps to this portico are flanked by massive blockings, surmounted by appropriate figures and trophies.

Over each column in the great frieze of the entablatures around the entire building are sculptured escutcheons (coats-of-arms of each State in the Union) surrounded by bronze civic wreaths, banded together by festoons of oak leaves, etc., all of which spring (each way) from the centre of the portico, where the coat-of-arms of the United States are emblazoned.

The statues surrounding the rotunda outside, under the colonnade, are all elevated upon pedestals, and will be those of the glorious signers of the Declaration of Independence.

Ascending the portico outside to the terrace level, a lofty vomitoria (doorway) 30 feet high, leads into the cella (rotunda gallery), 50 feet wide, 500 feet in circumference, and 68 feet high, with a colossal pillar in the centre 70 feet in diameter, around which the gallery sweeps.

Both sides of the gallery are divided into spaces by pilasters, elevated on a continued zocle or base 5 feet high, forming an order with its entablature 40 feet high, crowned by a vaulted ceiling 20 feet high, divided by radiating arched vaults, corresponding with the relative positions of the opposing pilasters, and inclosing deep sunken coffers enriched with paintings.

The spaces between the pilasters are sunk into niches for the reception of the statues of the fathers of the Revolution, contemporary with the immortal Washington; over which are large tablets to receive the national paintings commemorative of the battles and other scenes of that memorable period. Opposite to the entrance of this gallery, at the extremity of the great circular wall, is the grand niche for the reception of the statue of the " Father of his Country," elevated on its appropriate pedestal, and designated as *principal* in the group by its colossal proportions.

This spacious gallery and rotunda, which properly may be denominated the "National Pantheon," is lighted in four grand divisions from above, and, by its circular form, presents each subject decorating its walls in an interesting point of view and with proper effect, as the curiosity is kept up every moment, from the whole room not being presented to the eye at one glance, as in the case of a straight gallery.

Entering the centre pier through an arched way, you pass into a spacious circular area, and ascend with an easy grade, by a railway, to the grand terrace, 75 feet above the base of the monument. This terrace is 700 feet in circumference, 180 feet wide, inclosed by a colonnaded balustrade 15 feet high with its base and capping. The circuit of this grand terrace is studded with small temple-formed structures, constituting the cupolas of the lanterns, lighting the pantheon gallery below; by means of these little temples, from a gallery within, a bird's-eye view is had of the statues, etc., below.

In the centre of the grand terrace above described rises the lofty obelisk shaft of the monument, 70 feet square at the base and 500 feet high; at the foot of this shaft, and on its face, project four massive zocles 25 feet high, supporting so many colossal symbolic tripods of victory, 20 feet high, surmounted by facial columns with their symbols of authority. These zocle faces are embellished with inscriptions, which are continued around the entire base of the shaft, and occupy the surface of that part of the shaft between the tripods. On each face of the shaft above this is sculptured the four leading events in General Washington's eventful career, in basso relievo, and above this the shaft is perfectly plain to within 50 feet of its summit, where a simple star is placed emblematic of the glory which the name of Washington has attained.

The cost of all this, including obelisk and pantheon, was estimated at $1,122,000.

The idea of completing the pantheon was abandoned some years ago, and to erect the plain shaft only. When this is finished there will be a terrace at the base 200 feet square at the top, 17 feet high, terminating with slopes of two-thirds, with grass-plats and paved walks, and ascended by appropriate steps. The grounds around will also be improved and ornamented.

The Monument has had an eventful history. Half a century has passed away since the society was organized for the purpose of erecting it, and not a member of it is now living to enjoy the promised fulfilment of their hopes.

It appeared for many years as though the enterprise had proved a total failure; and now that the Monument has awakened to new life after its long slumber, there is an impatient desire upon the part of the boys and girls, who contributed so liberally towards its erection years ago, to see it completed. They have grown to manhood and womanhood, and are in turn telling their children of Washington and what they have done to help honor his memory.

A full and connected history has never been published, except in the Reports of Committees of Congress, and as these documents are accessible to comparatively few, a brief outline of its history may interest the reader and also prove valuable for reference in the future.

On the death of Washington, a joint Committee of the two Houses of Congress was appointed to consider the most suitable manner of paying honor to his memory.

Among the resolutions adopted in their report was one, "that a marble monument be erected by the United States, at the city of Washington, and that the family of General Washington be requested to permit his body to be deposited under it, and that the monument be so designed as to commemorate the great events of his military and political life."

On May 8, 1800, the Committee made a further report to the House of Representatives, on which the House passed a resolution, "that a mausoleum be erected to George Washington in the city of Washington."

January 1, 1801, the House passed a bill appropriating $200,000 for the erection of the mausoleum.

Nothing more seems to have been done in the matter for twenty years, and on January 15, 1824, Mr. Buchanan offered in the House of Representatives the following resolution: *"Resolved,* That a Committee be appointed whose duty it shall be to inquire in what manner the resolutions of Congress passed on the 24th of December, 1799, relative to the erection of a marble monument in the Capitol at the city of Washington, to commemorate the great events of the military and political life of General Washington may be best accomplished, and that they have leave to report by bill or otherwise."

The resolution was, after discussion, laid upon the table.

Nothing more was done by Congress, and as these resolutions remained unexecuted as late as 1833, some citizens of Washington, whose names were a passport to public confidence, formed in that year a voluntary association for erecting "a great National Monument to the memory of Washington at the seat of the Federal Government."

George Watterston, Esq., was the leading spirit in the undertaking, and the conception of the enterprise originated with him.

Chief Justice Marshall was the first president of the Washington National Monument Society, and held the position until the time of his death in 1835, when Ex-President Madison became president.

The proposed monument was intended to be raised by the voluntary contributions of the American people. The funds were to be collected in all parts of the United States, and in order that every person might have an opportunity of contributing, the contributions were limited to one dollar a year. This restriction was removed, though, in 1845.

The work progressed very slowly at first, but in 1836 $28,000 had been collected. This fund was judiciously invested, and in 1847 the interest and subsequent collections amounted to $87,000, and were deemed sufficient to justify the Society in beginning the erection.

Congress authorized the Society to erect the monument on one of the public reservations within the limits of the city of Washington not otherwise occupied. The present site was selected on account of its nearness to the river, where nothing could be built around to obstruct the view, and was convenient for the landing of stone, sand, and lime used in constructing it; and was also in full view of Mount Vernon, where reposed the ashes of the Chief. Another reason for selecting this site was that Washington himself had selected this particular spot for " a monument to the American Revolution," which, in the year 1795, was proposed should " be erected or placed at the permanent seat of government of the United States."

The anniversary of American Independence was

chosen as a fit day for laying the corner-stone of a monument to its hero; and on the 4th of July, 1848, under a bright sky, in the presence of the President and Vice-President of the United States, senators, representatives, heads of the executive departments, and other officers of the government; the corporate authorities of Washington, Georgetown, and Alexandria; military companies, associations of various kinds, delegations from States, Territories, and Indian tribes, and a countless multitude, Robert C. Winthrop, Speaker of the House of Representatives, pronounced an eloquent oration, and the corner-stone was laid.

In six years the obelisk was raised to 170 feet and $230,000 expended. The Society solicited contributions from the whole people, without distinction of party, sect, or creed; but the funds did not come in as rapidly as was hoped for, and in a short time it was obliged to suspend the work for want of means.

In 1854 the Board of Managers presented a memorial to Congress, giving a brief history of the enterprise, and stating that all recent efforts on their part to obtain means for completing the work had proved abortive; and they brought the subject before Congress for such action as it might deem proper.

The memorial was referred to a select committee, and on February 22, 1855, Mr. May, of Maryland, from the committee, made an able and eloquent report, and recommended a subscription of $200,000 by Congress " on behalf of the people of the United States, to aid the funds of the Society."

But on the very day of the presentment of this report the managers of the Society were superseded in their places by an unlawful election. The gentlemen engaged in the preparation of the history of the Society were very discreet and guarded in their allusions to this exciting time, and do not enter into particulars. It is well known, though, that the Know-Nothing party took violent possession of the Monument office and papers in 1855, and held them until 1858, when they were abandoned. A mob gathered about it at the time they took possession, and were so bent upon mischief and so bitter in their feelings against certain nationalities, that they seized the block of marble presented by the Pope, hammered it into pieces, and threw the fragments into the Potomac River.

The gentlemen interested in the enterprise, admonished by the experience of the past, decided to apply to Congress for a charter, and on February 22, 1859, an Act passed Congress, and was approved by the President on the 26th, incorporating "The Washington National Monument Society." By one of its provisions the President of the United States for the time being is *ex-officio* president of the Society, and the Governors of the several States respectively *ex-officio* its vice-presidents.

Only two courses of stone were laid between the years 1855–58, so that the monument had grown but four feet, and was 174 feet high when the Society regained possession.

In accordance with their former system the members invoked the aid of the States and Territories, and voluntary associations. The young State of California generously anticipated the appeal to her, and the Legislature passed an Act appropriating one thousand dollars annually in aid of the monument. This was never carried out, however, owing to the war and a lack of interest in the subject, but at the annual election of 1860, the citizens contributed at the polls $10,962.01, which was afterward paid to the Society through one of its friends.

"Each State," said the select Committee of the

House of Representatives in their report in 1855, "and two of the Territories of the Union have contributed a block of marble or stone, inscribed with its arms or some suitable inscription or device, and a great many others have been offered by various institutions and societies throughout the land; and several foreign governments have testified their desire to unite in this great work of humanity, intended to commemorate the virtue of its chief ornament and example."

As is well known, the storm of war which burst over our land in 1860 put a stop to all work upon the Monument, and it stood for fifteen or twenty years like a great tall, ugly factory chimney by the river side without anything more being done.

Congress then became stirred up on the subject and made an effort to finish it by the Centennial year, but found that would be impossible. The work, though, has gone on ever since, and there is a prospect now of having it completed in time for the next inaugural festivities.

The memorial stones presented by individuals, States, Territories, and foreign countries have, with the exception of that from Rome, been preserved and kept under cover. About forty of them have been built in with the structure, the others will be cut and properly fitted into niches upon the inner walls after the obelisk is completed.

These stones are extremely interesting, and one feels strangely moved while looking upon them; patriotic emotions swell the heart of even the most indifferent observer, and a little bit of the spirit of '76 takes possession of him in spite of himself.

One large block of marble bearing the device, in bas relief, of a school-house with a number of boys and girls on their way to school, is from 7500 children of Baltimore, Md. The date is 1855. There is another block from the Sunday schools of New York and one from the Sunday schools of Philadelphia. How touching! The little children of the country bringing their contributions to help rear a Monument to honor the memory of Washington!

There is a block of granite from the Cherokee Nation of Indians, sent in 1850; a block of granite from the battle-ground of Bunker Hill, and one from Braddock's field; also a large block of black marble from the battle-ground of Long Island, 1776, contributed in 1853. The stones from the several States and Territories bear appropriate inscriptions, and some are very handsomely carved. The block of marble from Louisiana has a pelican and her brood, and the inscription, "Ever faithful to the Constitution and the Union!" This stone, of course, was sent some time previous to the late war, and in view of the stirring and extraordinary events brought to light by the intervening years the motto reads strangely to-day. There is also a large marble slab from New Orleans, bearing the names of officers, privates, and honorary members of the Continental Guards of that city. This stone was sent in 1856, and when placed within the structure—as of course it will be—there will be a singular mingling of sentiment and reality, of true patriotism and false; for it is reasonable to suppose that nearly every member of the company entered the Confederate service. Men were too much in demand during the war for such a fine body of soldiers to be overlooked; and it is also reasonable to suppose that very many fell in defence of the Southern cause; but all this only shows what a wonderful people we are!

Vermont contributed a block of marble and Nevada a block of granite. The latter has the name of the State cut across the face in large letters and filled in with pure silver.

Pennsylvania sent a large block of marble ornamented with a sculptured spread eagle. There are a number of other stones from that State, from Odd-Fellows, Masons, and other societies, each bearing an appropriate device.

Ladies and gentlemen of the dramatic profession contributed a handsome block of marble with the head of Shakespeare in bas relief, and a suitable inscription.

Michigan sent a block of native copper weighing 2100 pounds, as "an emblem of her trust in the Union."

Altogether there have been more than a hundred stones contributed, and a number are from foreign countries.

There is a small block of granite from the original chapel built to William Tell in 1388 on Lake Lucerne, Switzerland, at the spot where he escaped from Gessler; a block of rough dark stone from Japan, and a similar one from China; a block of mottled marble from the Alexandrian Library, Egypt, and a block of variegated granite from the free town of Bremen.

Greece contributed an immense block of pure white marble, said to be a portion of the Parthenon at Athens. The inscription is in Greek.

The Governor and Commune of the Islands of Paros and Naxos presented a block of marble in 1855. In the same year the officers of the United States Steam Frigate "Saranac" presented a block of marble from the Temple of Esculapius, Island of Paros.

J. A. Lehman presented a small slab of marble with an ancient Egyptian head, which is supposed to have been carved between two and three thousand years ago, for the Temple erected in honor of Augustus on the banks of the Nile.

D. P. Heap, M.D., presented, nearly thirty years ago, a curious stone taken from the ruins of Carthage. It is one of the wonderful mosaics which have been uncovered there in modern times.

When Dom Pedro visited Washington during the Centennial year, he was very much interested in the Monument and these different stones, and was somewhat surprised to find that none had been sent from Brazil, and upon his return home ordered one to be prepared. It was received here in 1878, and although not at all handsome, makes up in size what it lacks in beauty. It is of granite, and will fill in considerable space if used in the structure.

The latest contribution from foreign countries is

17

from the King of Siam, which arrived the present year. It is a large slab of slate, one side covered with barnacles, as though it might have lain by the sea-shore for a time. It is interesting on account of the donor, but cannot be utilized for building pur- poses, and could not be considered ornamental under any circumstance.

The monument is now 350 feet high. The work is progressing very rapidly, but requires much labor and skill to build properly, and cannot be run up in a few days like the walls of an ordinary dwelling. The blocks of marble, which from below appear like large bricks, are really two feet wide, two feet high, and from five to seven feet long. They are taken up on trucks, which run upon rails laid directly from the workshop to the elevator. The elevator is worked by steam, and very strong and massive. I had the pleasure of going up the Monument one day not long since, and there were upon the elevator at the same time five other persons and a huge tub of broken stone for filling in the corners and uneven spaces.

The sensations experienced in going up are not pleasant. The space passed through is dark as mid- night and silent as the grave. The time occupied in making the ascent is from six to eight minutes, and a great relief is felt when the top is reached and you have air and light again. The view from the top is very fine, and repays one for the strain upon the nerves in going up.

For the protection of the workmen engaged in laying the heavy stones, strong iron arms project from the upper edge of the walls, to which is attached a heavy rope netting. Several have fallen over into this net, but have not been injured in any way.

When the obelisk is completed there will be an iron stairway to the top, and the interior lighted with electric lights.

XXVI.

SOLDIERS' HOME.

THE beautiful park surrounding the Soldiers' Home is the favorite drive of Washingtonians possessing stylish turnouts and spirited horses, and every pleasant afternoon hundreds of carriages pass through it. Its miles of hard, nicely graded roads, winding through velvety lawns, shady dells, and picturesque views, are just the thing for the display of fine equipages, and at the same time afford a pleasant, cool retreat from the dust and glare of the city.

The Home was established in 1852 for the benefit of old and disabled soldiers of the regular army, and while the grounds are in one sense a public park, they really belong to the soldiers and are kept in order by them.

To General Winfield Scott belongs the honor of suggesting the institution, and in recognition of his services a fine bronze statue has been erected upon the lawn facing the Capitol. The money for the first outlay came from Mexico. During the war with that country and after the capture of their Capital, the citizens took refuge upon the house-tops and mercilessly fired upon our soldiers, and for this outrageous mode of warfare General Scott levied a tax upon them of $100,000, which was paid. General Scott transmitted the amount to the Secretary of War, with the suggestion that it be used for the purpose above named, which was done.

Commissioners were appointed, under the direction of Congress, to select a suitable site and have a building erected, and the present attractive retreat is the result. The first piece of land purchased comprised 256 acres, and with the mansion upon it cost $57,000. This land was the property of G. W. Riggs, Esq., and the house, his country residence, has been very substantially built and provided with the conveniences of bath, furnace, piazzas, etc. President Hayes occupied this house the summer he spent at the Home, and President Arthur spent the greater part of last summer there.

In 1853 three acres were added to the original tract, and in 1855 three more.

In 1872 a very valuable addition was made by the

purchase of "Harewood," the country seat of W. W. Corcoran, Esq. This property consisted of 191 acres, much of it highly improved, and with a subsequent purchase of forty odd acres, increased the original tract to 502 acres.

The main building is of marble; Norman in design, and, with the additional dormitory, capable of accommodating four hundred persons.

The Home is supported by a tax of $12\frac{1}{2}$ cents per month upon all soldiers of the army, collected every two months; all the unclaimed effects of deceased soldiers, and also whatever is due deserters at the time of desertion; forfeitures and the fines imposed by courts-martial.

Upon fifty-five acres of the land vegetables are raised for the use of the inmates, and grass cut from two hundred and fifty acres.

The old soldiers have a very comfortable time, and their quarters could not well be made any more attractive. There is a fine hospital, a beautiful little chapel of Seneca stone, and a library and reading-room. Some of the men are unable to read and some do not care to take the trouble, and a custom has grown up at the Home of having one of the men, who has a good voice and who reads well, to read the daily papers to the others every morning. He takes his station in a summer-house in front of the main building when the weather is pleasant, and the old soldiers, with their lighted pipes, gather around him and listen. For this service he receives about seven dollars a month extra pay.

President Buchanan and President Lincoln were both in the habit of summering at the Home, but they did not occupy the same cottage now used by the President.

The park will compare favorably with those of other cities. It is far more beautiful than Central Park; it is not as large as Fairmount Park of Philadelphia, and lacks the picturesque Schuylkill River, which adds so much to the latter, but I think some of the views are quite as fine as that from George's Hill, Fairmount.

XXVII.

ENVIRONS.

TO do full justice to the environs of Washington would require the pen of the historian, the novelist, and the poet, for it seems to me every hill-top, every mansion-house, and almost every farm-house within a radius of ten miles has a peculiar story of its own. It may be of love, or war, or of some individual greatly distinguished in the political history of the country; and a simple mention of the facts can give but a faint idea of the interesting stories connected with them.

Upon the heights right across the river is Arlington House, which visitors to the Capital always regard as one of the chief points of interest, and are always ready to listen to anything relating to it whether of the past or present.

The history of the estate is interesting. The land is a part of the tract known as the Howson Grant, made during the reign of Charles II., and granted by Sir William Berkeley, Governor of Virginia, to Robert Howson, in consideration of having transported a number of persons into the colony. There were six thousand acres of it, and on the 13th day of October, 1669, Howson conveyed the grant to John Alexander for six hogsheads of tobacco. The tract extended from the Long Bridge to some distance below Alexandria, and the latter place was named in compliment to the owner.

The property descended from father to children, and in course of time became divided into several tracts. John Parke Custis purchased a portion from Gerard Alexander, and there is a story current in the family about the transaction worth repeating.

It seems that negotiations had been pending for some time, and one Sunday morning Mr. Custis and Mr. Alexander attended service at Falls Church, Virginia. After service Mr. Alexander invited Mr. Custis—as the custom was at that time—to go home with him and dine. The invitation was accepted, and after a comfortable dinner some conversation took place about the land, and Mr. Custis wishing to close the bargain offered his check or note in payment. Mrs. Alexander, who was a strict church

woman, overheard the conversation, and spoke up
very decidedly, saying: "We can have no business
transacted here on the Lord's day." Her husband
turned to his guest and said: "The women rule here,
so put back your check." The afternoon was spent in
pleasant conversation, and the evening drawing near,
Mr. Custis went out to mount his horse to return to
his home. His host followed him to the horse-block,
and some further conversation took place about the
property, and the check was again offered and this
time accepted. The next day Mr. Alexander learned
to his sorrow that Congress had the Saturday previous passed a law in regard to the Continental money
which made the payment he had received, instead of
a fine price for his land, almost a total loss.

This story may not be strictly true, but it is well
known that Mr. Custis purchased the land, and that
in 1778 General Alexander executed the following
instrument :—

"It is this day agreed between Gerard Alexander,
of Fairfax County, of the one part, and Robert
Adams, for John Parke Custis of the other, that the
said Gerard Alexander will comply with the said
John Parke Custis, his heirs and assigns forever, all
the land he is entitled to between the line called

North Six (in Howson's patent agreeable to a plat
and recovery made lately in the General Court) and
Potomac River, supposed to be 1,000 acres, for the
sum of eleven thousand pounds currency. Possession
will be given on the 25th of December, 1778, for the
performance of which the above parties have bound
themselves in one thousand pounds.

> GERARD ALEXANDER,
> ROBERT ADAMS.

Witness: PHILIP ALEXANDER.

FAIRFAX, December 25, 1778.

Then received of John Parke Custis the sum of eleven thousand
pounds, Virginia currency, in full, for a tract of land, supposed one
thousand acres, lying on Potomac River, and in the county of
Fairfax.

(Signed)   GERARD ALEXANDER."

In the will of Robert Alexander, who was a brother
of Gerard, made in 1793, is the following: "Item : I
give to my son Robert and his heirs forever, one-
half of the land which I formerly sold to the late
Mr. John P. Custis, and upon which I now live." . . .
This land was probably another part of the original
tract, and was either not paid for by Mr. Custis, or
was repurchased by Mr. Alexander.

The mansion was built about the beginning of the
century by G. W. P. Custis, son of John Parke Cus-

tis. He must have been a very young man at the time, and could have scarcely attained his majority, having been born in 1781 at Mount Airy, Md. Young men in those days must have been more mature at twenty-one than they are at the present time, for such an undertaking as the planning and erection of an imposing residence like "Arlington House" would overwhelm the average youth of to-day. The mansion was designed from drawings of the Temple at Pæstum, near Naples. There is a main building 60 feet wide, and two wings, each 40 feet wide, giving a front of 140 feet. The portico across the front is 25 feet deep and 60 feet long, and supported by eight large columns. There are many fine old mansions scattered through Virginia, relics of colonial times, and this house is a fair sample. They were all famous for hospitality, and for the generous style of living of their respective owners. Mr. Custis was not a whit behind his ancestors in this respect, and Arlington was for many years the favorite visiting place for both old and young of Washington and vicinity.

He was a patron of agriculture, and bestowed much attention upon fine stock, and, becoming interested in the rearing of fine sheep, in 1803 inaugurated an annual convention for the promotion of agriculture, etc., which was known throughout the country by the title of "Arlington Sheep Shearings." They were held on the slope in front of the mansion, near a spring which gushed out from beneath the roots of a grand old oak tree.

In *Niles's Weekly Register* of May 23, 1812, one of these anniversaries is described as follows: " The most liberal attention was paid by Mr. Custis to the accommodation and convenience of the company, in producing a profusion of necessary refreshments, and in furnishing books for the amusement of those not immediately engaged in the business of the day. The company, consisting of several members of the National Legislature, some French gentlemen of distinction, and a number of respectable characters from the States of Virginia and Maryland and the District of Columbia, repaired to the marque prepared for the occasion, when, at half-past three, they sat down to an elegant dinner, consisting principally of a great variety of fish (served up in various and tasteful style) furnished from the adjoining river.

" The day was uncommonly mild for the season. The awning, composed of the canvas which had so often sheltered the immortal founder of the liberties

of his country, beautifully ornamented with festoons
of laurel, and a striking likeness of the General suspended over the foot of the table, altogether inspired
feelings of unutterable expression."

Mr. Custis was not entirely successful in his sheep
rearing venture. By dogs and thieves his fine flock
of merinos was finally reduced to two sheep, that
delighted to wander at their own sweet will over the
grassy slopes and heights of Arlington.

The hospitality, for which the mansion was so
famous, did not cease at the death of Mr. Custis.
He bequeathed it to his daughter, Mrs. Lee, wife of
General Robert E. Lee, the well-known Confederate
leader, and at the beginning of the war they were
residing there. At that time the house was a charming country home; and apart from the refined,
agreeable inmates, stored with so many objects of
historical interest, one esteemed it a privilege to be
entertained there.

Portraits of Washington, Mrs. Washington, beautiful Nelly Custis, Colonel Daniel Parke, Governor
Will Byrd, and other ancestors on both sides of the
family adorned the walls; valuable china and silver
plate graced the sideboard; antique furniture and precious heirlooms were scattered through the rooms; in

the hall hung the antlers of the deer killed at Mount
Vernon in 1799, by order of Washington, for the entertainment of a favored guest, and afterward served
up in his own dining-room, and the library contained
valuable books, letters, and historical documents.
Everything combined to make an attractive home,
and it is painful to dwell upon the great change which
has come to the grand old homestead by reason of
the storm of war that raged so many months around
it. Mr. Custis in making his will devised his property to Mrs. Lee during her natural life, and at her
death to descend to her son, and was to remain, pictures, plate, furniture, books, etc., unchanged and entire at Arlington, and descend to his latest posterity.

How little did he anticipate or realize what a fear-
ful storm was brewing even at that time, and the
changes to follow in its train.

The family has been broken up. The parents are
dead, the household treasures scattered or destroyed
beyond restoration; the walls of the mansion, once
bright with interesting family portraits, are now hung
with plots of the adjoining graveyard showing the
exact locality of each grave, and the hall resounds
with the footsteps of strangers. The beautiful parlors and spacious ball-room, where youth and beauty

mingled in the social dance, keeping time with lively strains of music, are now silent and deserted.

When the war broke out Mrs. Lee followed the fortunes of her husband and went South, taking her jewels and valuable silver with her and leaving the house in charge of servants. It was immediately occupied by the Government, and the hills and fields around became one great camping ground. Being the property of a minor, the estate could not be seized under the Confiscation Act, but the Government continued to hold it in default of payment of taxes. After the war ended this involved a lawsuit, which after pending several years was finally decided in favor of Mr. Lee. The latter has recently conveyed the property to the Government for the sum of $150,000, as he does not care to return to it in its changed condition.

As is well known, the slopes around the mansion are now one vast graveyard, where are resting the remains of twelve thousand Union soldiers. I say twelve thousand, but beside the graves there is a handsome mausoleum in one part of the grounds, beneath which are gathered the bones of thousands more—bones collected from the various battle-fields, and so far beyond all chance of identification it was impossible to decide whether they belonged to friend or foe. They are quietly resting together, and the monument is inscribed "Unknown."

The first grave made in the cemetery was for a young man who had enlisted under a fictitious name, and when death approached, refused to tell his attendants his real name or anything about his family, and requested that his tombstone be simply marked "*Mustered out.*"

Along the walks by the graves have been erected a number of iron tablets, upon which are inscribed in white letters quotations from the touchingly beautiful poem of Colonel Theodore O'Hara, written for and delivered upon the occasion of the re-interment at Frankfort of the Kentucky soldiers who fell in the battle of Buena Vista.

A strange coincidence, that the words of a dead Southerner, written for the funeral ceremonies of Southern soldiers, should have been selected to express the sentiments of the Northern survivors of the late struggle over the sad fate of their comrades!

The following are some of the quotations:—

> "On Fame's eternal camping ground
> Their silent tents are spread;
> And glory guards with solemn round
> The bivouac of the dead."

18

"Rest on, embalmed and sainted dead,
   Dear as the blood ye gave;
No impious footstep here shall tread
   The herbage of your grave."

"No rumor of the foe's advance
   Now swells upon the wind;
No troubled thought at midnight haunts
   Of loved ones left behind."

"The neighing troop, the flashing blade,
   The bugle's stirring blast;
The charge, the dreadful cannonade,
   The din and shout are past."

"The muffled drum's sad roll has beat
   The soldier's last tattoo;
No more on life's parade shall meet
   That brave and fallen few."

The tomb of Lieutenant John R. Meigs, son of Major-General Meigs, Quartermaster-General, now in the cemetery, is very interesting. This gallant young officer was killed by guerillas near Harrison-burg, Va., while making a military survey in his capacity of Chief Engineer of the Army of the Shen-andoah.

The tomb consists of a pedestal of black marble upon which is laid, sculptured in bronze, the body of the young man in precisely the same position as found after death. The form is reduced in size, and represents him lying upon his back dressed in uniform with overcoat on and thrown open. One hand is clasped upon his breast, the other hangs by the side, a pistol near it, apparently having fallen from it as his eyes closed in death. The ground around bears the impress of horses' hoofs.

The tomb of Mr. Custis and wife are also in the cemetery.

There are a small number of Southern soldiers buried within the inclosure, and nothing shows more clearly the re-established fraternal feeling between the two sections than the fact that no difference is now made in the annual decoration of graves.

> " From the silence of sorrowful hours
>   The desolate mourners go,
> Lovingly laden with flowers
>   Alike for the friend and the foe.
> Under the sod and the dew,
>   Waiting the judgment day ;
> Under the roses, the Blue,
>   Under the lilies, the Gray."

While upon the one hand the changes in the estate have been very sad, upon the other they have been beneficial. Under the care of the Government the place has been made to bud and blossom as the rose, and when I last visited it during the month of roses,

was charming beyond description. The interior of
the mansion is about the same as it has been for
many years—silent and desolate! but the exterior
and the grounds have been transformed into visions
of beauty. Across the west end of the house a luxuriant vine has climbed to the roof and the beautiful
purple blossoms hang in great clusters. The small
houses, near which were originally negro quarters,
are completely covered with the Virginia creeper.

After the Southern fashion, the vegetable garden
occupies the space one side of the mansion and the
flower garden the other. The latter has been inclosed by an arbor-vitæ hedge, and laid out in beds
and walks bordered with box-wood. The beds were
brilliant with roses and other flowers. The grounds
have been surrounded by a low brick wall and provided with handsome gateways.

The place possesses many natural beauties in the
way of shady dells, grassy slopes, and picturesque
ravines, which have been largely added to by the
hand of art.

The underbrush has been cut away from the lofty
oaks and clumps of evergreens interspersed.

The hill-sides have been terraced, and smoothly
gravelled roads made to wind around them. Foun-

tains and vases and ornamental shrubbery have been added to the parterres of flowers near the house, and the turf is kept in exquisite order. Altogether, the property is very much changed and improved, and those who saw it only during the war period would scarcely recognize it now.

GEORGETOWN can hardly be classed with the environs of Washington now, for it is a part of the city and known as West Washington, the names of the streets and numbers on the houses being merely a continuation of those of the city proper.

The old town, though, is extremely interesting. The ancestral homes of many of the most prominent families of the District are located upon its ancient streets or upon the surrounding heights.

It dates back to Colonial times, having been founded in 1751, and was a place of considerable importance long before Washington was thought of as the site of the future Capital. At the close of the Revolutionary War, and for many years after, it was celebrated for its refined, cultivated society and the business enterprise of its citizens.

In "ye olden time" it was quite a gay place.

There seems to have been a rage for building fine houses, and the style of living was luxurious. Every planter and man of wealth had his handsome coach horses and racers, and both gentlemen and ladies lived and dressed in fine old English style. Balls and dinners, cock fighting and horse racing were freely indulged in. After the seat of Government was removed to Washington many members of Congress made their homes in Georgetown, as the hotels and boarding-houses were much superior to those of the former place. A coach-and-four was used for transferring the distinguished legislators from their hotel to the Capitol.

The first sale of Government building lots took place at Georgetown October 17, 1791, and was attended by a large number of purchasers from all parts of the country.

The "fall races" were as much a feature of Georgetown at the beginning of the century as they are of Washington now, and Congress was quite as willing to adjourn early in order to attend them as are the members of the present Congress.

An Englishman by the name of Janson, travelling in America in 1803, upon his return to England wrote a book describing what he saw there, and among other things he says : " In November in each year there are horse races at the Capital of America. I happened to arrive just at this time, on horseback, at Georgetown, which is about two miles from the race-ground, and at an early hour proceeded to the turf. Though the day was raw, cold, and threatening to rain or snow, there were abundance of ladies decorated as if for a ball. In this year (1803) Congress was summoned early by President Jefferson upon the contemplated purchase of Louisiana, and to pass a bill in order to facilitate his election again as President. Many scores of American legislators, who are all allowed six dollars a day, besides their travelling expenses, went on foot from the Capitol, above four English miles, to attend the sport; nay, it is an indisputable fact that the houses of Congress adjourned at a very early hour to indulge the members for this purpose. It rained during the course, and thus the law-makers of the country were driven into the booths, and thereby compelled to eat and pay for what was there called a dinner, while their contemplated meal remained untouched at their respective boarding-houses. Economy is the order of the day in the Jeffersonian administration of that country, and the members pretend to avail themselves of it even in their personal expenses."

In 1800 the Chesapeake and Ohio Canal was completed around the Great and Little Falls, and the business of the town was very important. The Potomac River was navigable at that time for large ships and other vessels, and as late as the year 1820 eight ships, thirteen brigs, and nine schooners cleared from the port for foreign ports. Large quantities of tobacco were shipped to the West Indies and other countries; and the traffic in grain was very brisk.

The foundation of the princely fortune afterwards gained by the philanthropist, George Peabody, was laid in Georgetown, and in recognition of his success in business there he endowed a library which bears his name.

Georgetown College is the oldest Roman Catholic institution of learning in the country, and dates back to 1789. It is situated upon a high hill, the last in the range inclosing the amphitheatre in which the city of Washington is located, and commands a magnificent view of the river and surrounding country. In the rear of the building the rugged country, lofty oaks, and thick undergrowth, present all the beauty and wildness of a forest scene, while in front is all the hurry and bustle of a large city. On the south side the Potomac emerges from its narrow channel and threads its way around pretty islands, grassy slopes, and wooded bluffs on its hurried journey seaward. In the distance the fertile fields of Maryland and Virginia stretch out for many miles. The College was founded by John Carroll, afterwards Archbishop of Baltimore, and a cousin of Charles Carroll of Carrollton. He was born at Upper Marlboro', Prince George's County, Md.

Father Carroll took his final vows as Professed Father of the Society of Jesus in 1771, and on the suppression of the Order in 1773, was obliged to fly to England, but returned shortly after to Maryland and resided on Rock Creek, a few miles from Georgetown.

It had long been his wish to establish an academy in Maryland, and in the year 1789, in spite of many embarrassments, his efforts were crowned with success.

The old estates of the Jesuits in Maryland still remained in their possession after the suppression of the Society, and from the revenues of these or from sales of lands, the College was mainly built before the Society was restored.

It was the beauty of the situation which led him to select the present site, and not its proximity to the Capital, for at that time it had not been decided where the Capital should be permanently located. The first building is still standing, and forms a part of the south row.   The north building was commenced in 1794, but, from want of funds, not completed till 1808.

At the time of the destruction of the Capitol by the British after the battle of Bladensburg, the Government decided to take this building for the convenience of Congress, as it was the largest in the vicinity ; but the speedy erection of another Capitol obviated the necessity for doing so.

Upon the occasion of one of General Washington's visits to the College in 1797, he was received with a poetical address by Robert Walsh, then sixteen years old, afterwards United States Consul to Paris.

According to tradition, Washington rode up unattended, hitched his horse to the palings, and was warmly received by Professor Matthews, who subsequently became President of the College.   Since then the Presidents have been in the habit of attending the Commencement exercises, and usually award the diplomas and medals.

The first student at the academy cut his name—William Gaston—upon a window pane, where it still remains. He afterward became the eminent jurist and statesman of North Carolina, and, strange to say, a son of his granddaughter is a pupil at the College at the present time.

The late war had a very blighting effect upon the prosperity of the institution, and although never entirely closed during that time, the attendance dwindled down from three hundred students to a mere handful, and has never since been up to the former standard.

When the news reached Georgetown of the bombardment of Fort Sumter and the call of President Lincoln for troops, the students, like many mature citizens, were seized with a panic and hurried off to their respective homes, leaving scarcely one hundred at the college. A part of the building was then taken for barracks for the soldiers pouring into Washington day and night. On Saturday the 4th of May, 1861, the Sixty-ninth New York Regiment marched into the grounds and occupied the south building—the professors and students taking quarters in the infirmary.

This regiment remained several weeks and then passed over into Virginia.

The Seventy-ninth New York, a Scotch regiment, then took possession and remained until the 4th of July. The scholastic exercises were kept up, during the occupation of the building by the soldiers, notwithstanding the fact that it was necessary to give the watchword to pass from one part of the house to another.

After the second battle of Bull Run, in 1862, which occurred about thirty miles west of the college, it was turned into a hospital and everything unsettled for another year. The school, however, was continued, and after hospitals were erected in different parts of the city the soldiers evacuated the college and it passed from under military control.

The building has been added to lately by the addition of a handsome new front, commenced in 1871 and now nearly completed. It is 312 feet long. The walls are built solidly of blue gneiss rock from the upper Potomac, with bluish-gray Ohio freestone and North River blue-stone for the cut work. Every convenience in the way of heating, lighting, and water has been added, and the structure is spacious and substantial.

The college has a very fine library, embracing upwards of 30,000 volumes, and among them some very curious and costly books. There are two volumes of the Odes of Horace printed from copper plates, which are very elaborately illustrated, and are claimed to have cost $18,000.

Among the ancient books is a law book printed in 1483, a Roman Missal of 1630, a Latin Bible of 1479, and said to be the oldest book in the country, an illuminated manuscript copy of the "Epistles of St. Paul," Book of Psalms of 1586, a book written in Hindostanee, and one in Irish. Also a very small Mahometan Prayer-book, taken by Decatur from a soldier at Tripoli.

A large oval table, in the centre of the room, was once the property of Lord Baltimore, and presented to the college in 1875.

On the heights of Georgetown are many old and aristocratic mansions, surrounded with fine grounds filled with choice flowers and shrubbery, indicating a refined and cultivated taste on the part of their respective owners.

One of the most interesting of these is "Tudor Place," owned and occupied at present by a niece of G. W. P. Custis. The house was built in 1812, and is very large and attractive. The first floor is so arranged that the rooms can be thrown into one grand saloon by means of sliding doors. The front windows command a magnificent view of the city and distant hills. The grounds are quite extensive and well shaded by large forest trees. The walks are bordered with hedges of box-wood, so old and thick that they measure nearly a yard across the top.

On the northern slope of the heights is Oak Hill Cemetery, remarkable for the natural beauty of the spot, what has been done by the hand of art, and for the number of distinguished persons buried there. The hillside has been terraced down to the very edge of Rock Creek, which winds around the base, and the water making a small fall quite near sounds like soft, sad music in the air. The cemetery, originally but ten acres in extent, was the gift of W. W. Corcoran, Esq., whose wife and daughter are resting there beneath a very elegant white marble mausoleum.

Chief Justice Chase is buried there, also Secretary Stanton, General Reno, Commodore Morris, and other public men; and it is now the final resting place of John Howard Payne, where beneath an elegant monument his remains have found a "Home," after a slumber of more than thirty years in the Protestant Cemetery of St. George, at Tunis. Bringing his remains back to his native land and having them reburied beneath the grand old oaks he once loved so well, is another instance of the noble generosity of Mr. Corcoran.

Mr. Corcoran knew and admired Mr. Payne at the time he was residing in Washington, and when he died in a foreign land, cherished a hope he might one day bring back his remains; but many more important matters occupied his mind and hands during the intervening years and the wish was not carried out. · Strange to say, one day, during the year 1882, upon hearing the notes of the wonderful song —which has given Mr. Payne a name destined to live as long as the English language shall be spoken —his heart was touched by the plaintive strain as it had never been before, and the wish assumed definite shape, and he decided to begin at once the first move in the matter, viz: a correspondence with the State Department.

There was much delay and much red tape to be

disposed of before the final arrangements for the removal and reburial could be made; but Mr. Corcoran spared neither pains nor expense to make the obsequies solemn and impressive.

I had the pleasure of witnessing the scene, and it was both beautiful and interesting. The ceremonies were attended with considerable pomp, and it was a rare privilege to see the group of distinguished men participating. President Arthur and his Cabinet, General Hancock, General Sherman, Justice Matthews, ex-Justice Strong, Bishop Pinckney, Professor Welling, and members of the Diplomatic Corps, joined the procession, which entered the cemetery preceded by the Marine Band, playing in a low key, "Home, Sweet Home."

Suitable religious forms were then observed, and afterward a poem and an interesting oration delivered, followed by a hymn sung by one hundred voices.

About one mile from Georgetown, on the Tennallytown Road, stands a very old mansion which has borne the storms and sunshine of nearly one hundred years. It is located upon the brow of a hill, and from the porch one gets a fine view of the city of

Washington, which lies in the valley away off below. Wonderful changes have taken place in the valley since the corner-stone of the old house was laid, of which it has been a silent witness, and the place forms an interesting link between the past and the present. It was built about the year 1786 by General Uriah Forrest, and there is a tradition in the family that General Washington selected the site. A very good selection he made, too.

The plantation was originally very large, and extended from Pierce's Mill to Georgetown. General Forrest was a distinguished officer in the Revolutionary War, and married a beautiful Maryland lady. Judge Philip Barton Key, the uncle of Francis Scott Key, author of the "Star Spangled Banner," married a sister of Mrs. Forrest, and the two families so closely connected by marriage became neighbors— Judge Key purchasing a portion of the land and establishing a handsome home near by.

This old homestead—interesting as it is on account of its great age and being associated with so many distinguished persons—has had a new interest lent to it of late years by reason of the romantic and extraordinary experiences of a granddaughter of General Forrest.

19

This lady was born and reared in the old home and has frequently returned to it for shelter and comfort when weighed down by the strange and perplexing trials which have surrounded her.

The story of her life reads more like romance than real life, and the history of several noted individuals is closely linked with hers.

About the year 1860, or maybe a little later, there was attached to the Mexican Legation at Washington, in the capacity of secretary, a very accomplished Mexican gentleman. He became a frequent visitor at "Rosedale," and in course of time fell very much in love with Miss Alice Green, the young lady referred to. He offered her his hand, and as she reciprocated his affection, they were in a short time married. The gentleman was Don Angel de Iturbide, a son of the ill-fated Emperor of Mexico, Don Augustin the First.

The history of that sovereign is very sad. After being deprived of his throne by his enemies he was banished from the country and with him his family also. The family remained in England for a number of years, and it was while living there that young Iturbide acquired a knowledge of the English language which fitted him for the position he afterwards held at Washington.

A son was born to the couple and the happiness of the young mother seemed complete. About the year 1864, and while the civil war still raged in the United States, Maximilian, of Austria, as is well known, attempted, with the aid of Napoleon, to establish himself upon the throne of Mexico. How well he succeeded in doing so is now a matter of history.

The Mexicans did not receive him very heartily, and his hold upon the people was always vague and uncertain. He was anxious to make himself acceptable to them, and also to conciliate the Iturbides, whom he found were still very dear to a large number, and Carlotta, his wife, was constantly urging him to make use of every means within his reach to win their confidence and regard.

Having learned of the young son of Don Angel, and having no children of his own, he conceived the idea of adopting the child as his heir to the throne, and accordingly sent for the parents.

He made the proposal to them, and promised that he would provide for the education of young Don Augustin, and would rear him as his own child. As a further inducement to the parents, a liberal pension was to be secured to all the older members of the Iturbide family.

The mother, dazzled by the brilliant prospects held out to her child, and no doubt ambitious to be the mother of an emperor, in a moment of weakness yielded, and gave her consent to the arrangement, and the child was given up to Maximilian. A paper was then drawn and duly signed by all the adult Iturbides at the time in Mexico.

As soon as the Emperor obtained possession of this paper, he notified the parents that they were expected to quit Mexico immediately, and they prepared to leave the country. Arriving at Pueblo, on the journey, the mother for the first time realizing what she had done became almost frantic from grief, and in her despair determined at all hazards to return to the capital and take back her child.

She retraced her steps to the City of Mexico, and upon arriving sought the house of a friend. The next morning she wrote to Maximilian, told him what she was suffering, and implored him to restore to her her child. He did not reply, but sent a message leading her to believe an interview would be granted her the following day.

At an early hour the next morning an officer

called with a message from their Majesties, requesting her to come to the Palace to talk the matter over. She dressed herself very carefully for the expected interview, and, after the custom of ladies in that country, threw over her head and shoulders a black lace mantilla. Descending to the door, she found one of the imperial carriages waiting, and with a troubled heart took her seat.

Instead of being driven directly to the Palace, she soon found she was being whirled rapidly through the streets to the edge of the city. She remonstrated with the officer, but it had no effect, and on the outskirts of the city was taken by force from the carriage, thrust into a diligence, and, under the charge of another officer, driven for two days and one night back to Puebla.

The rain poured down incessantly during the journey, and she had no other protection for her head from the dampness and cold than the lace mantilla. The family were then ordered to leave Mexico by the next steamer.

Upon arriving in Washington Mrs. Iturbide sought the aid of Secretary Seward in regaining possession of her child, but Mr. Seward declined to interfere in such a delicate matter.

She then sailed for France, and went directly to Paris to seek an interview with Louis Napoleon, and to ask him to intercede for her with the Emperor of Mexico. But he also declined to interfere, and there was nothing more left her but to calmly await the progress of events.

Maximilian's star of popularity, never very bright, now began to grow dim, and at times threatened to become lost to view entirely. Soon after the unhappy mother arrived in Paris searching for some one to help her recover her lost treasure, the unhappy wife of the Emperor also appeared, seeking aid to restore the waning fortunes of her husband.

Mrs. Iturbide at once sought an interview with her, and although painful and rather unsatisfactory, it was not altogether fruitless, and she succeeded in making some slight impression upon the womanly heart of the Empress. Without giving any definite promise to restore the child, she directed the mother to address a note to the Emperor, advised her what to say to him, and what means to make use of to have the note reach him.

This note may have had the desired effect, or Maximilian may have found the boy could be of no further use to him, or the storm which had been gathering for many months had already burst upon him ; at any rate, he decided to restore him to his parents.

The mother was directed to go to Havana to meet him, and finally, after a separation of more than two years, had the joy of clasping him in her arms once more.

Don Augustin is now a man. He has been carefully educated in the best schools and colleges of this country and Europe. His father died about ten years ago, and the mother and son are at present enjoying each other's society at the old homestead where she spent the years of her girlhood.

Emperors may come and emperors may go, but she does not care for them, for she has learned from bitter experience that the possession and love of her child is worth more to a true mother's heart than the prospective crowns of all Christendom.

Spent the morning at BLADENSBURG. It is very strange, but if one happens to drop a hint about a contemplated visit to this old town, they may be sure of seeing a derisive smile upon the face of the hearer, usually followed by all sorts of ironical suggestions. Why it is so is not apparent. It is a pretty little town nestled among the hills, rather old-fashioned, I admit, and rather quiet and sleepy; but these are the very things which make it attractive; and apart from the natural beauties, has so many delightful old houses, historical memories, and interesting stories, that a visit is thoroughly enjoyable.

The town was settled about 1750, and took its name from Thomas Bladen, brother-in-law of 5th Lord Baltimore and Governor of Maryland in 1742.

The land originally belonged to the Calvert estate, which at that time was called Yarrow, and sixty acres were deeded to the town. It was a place of considerable importance in the latter part of the last century. At that time Washington was of no consequence whatever, and Bladensburg and Georgetown had all the trade of the surrounding country. The land was very productive, and large quantities of grain and tobacco were raised and sold.

The Eastern Branch, upon which the town is situated, at the head of tidewater, was a very different stream some years ago from what it is at present; large sloops and schooners ascended as far as Bladensburg and took in and discharged their cargoes at the wharves. There were several large warehouses in the town, and the merchants were busily

engaged buying and selling tobacco and other com-
modities. As late as the year 1832 the schooner
" Red Rover" left the port laden with ninety hogsheads of tobacco; at Alexandria and Georgetown
the cargoes were usually transferred to ships, and
from there taken to foreign countries. In this way
a brisk trade was opened with Scotland and other
countries, and the wonderful stories of the product-
iveness of this part of America induced many of the
Scotch to come over and settle there.

The former name of the Eastern Branch was Anacostia, from a tribe of Indians, whose wigwams
were at one time scattered along its banks. There
is something very singular about the filling up of
the stream ; to see it now, one can scarcely imagine
any boat larger than a canoe had ever ascended it ;
at some points it is so narrow, one might easily leap
across, and in some places so shallow that it is
nothing more than a sparkling brook rushing mer-
rily over a pebbly bed.

Bladensburg was at one time quite a fashionable
place ; the celebrated Spa Spring attracting many
persons to it. The belles and beaux from the surrounding country often met in the ball-room to

spend the evening in the mazy dance and enjoy flir-
tations beneath the soft light of the silvery moon.

Before the days of railroads it was a post-town,
and the old inn, so popular as a stopping-place at
that time, is still standing. One can fancy the
scenes to be witnessed daily upon that long porch,
where planters, merchants, politicians, and here and
there an African face were awaiting the arrival of
the stage, and the pompous Jehus, with a blast from
the bugle and crack of the whip, gracefully handling
the ribbons, would dash up in grand style to the
door.

The event of August 24, 1814, made the place
historical, and the disastrous defeat of the Americans that day left the Capital at the mercy of the
enemy.

I talked with the oldest inhabitant, who pointed
out the exact spot where the battle was fought, the
abutments of the old bridge over which the British
crossed into the town, the house used by them as a
hospital, the chimney in which a cannon-ball is em-
bedded, and many other interesting things.

There are a number of the original houses still
standing; their sloping roofs, tiny windows, and

huge brass knockers upon the front door, giving evidence of their great age.

On Sand Street there is an old brick house into which Sir William Wood was carried, severely wounded, the day of the battle. Near by is the decayed stump of a large tree, all that is left of a graceful willow, under the shade of which he was wont to sit during his convalescence. He became so much attached to the tree, that upon his return to England he carried a twig with him to plant near his own home, but found American roots planted in English soil did not flourish as well as English roots planted upon American soil, for it did not grow. For many years after that time, whenever any of his countrymen visited Washington, they always made a pilgrimage to Bladensburg for the purpose of looking upon the old battle-ground and visiting the houses where their wounded had been cared for. They too cut twigs from the old tree, and finally the weight of years bowed its head to the ground.

Sir William returned to America some years after the war, and spent a week at "Blenheim," the charming country residence of Mr. L. This fine old mansion dates back to 1800, and is situated about half a mile from the town. It is surrounded by a beautiful lawn shaded by towering oaks, a part of the primeval forest.

There was a duel fought many years ago, directly opposite the house, between Mr. Gardiner and Mr. Campbell, and the latter falling wounded, was carried into the mansion and carefully nursed.

Another fine mansion in the vicinity is "Cloud-land," which is supposed to have been built by a Scotch merchant named Dick, as he occupied the house for many years. An iron plate in the fireplace of the reception room bears the date 1769. The view from the portico is particularly fine, and there are a number of interesting reminiscences connected with the homestead. Captain Hunter, of the United States Navy, lived there at the beginning of the late war. He resigned his position to take up the Southern cause, leaving his beautiful home and many rare and valuable articles collected while an officer in the Navy—among them the first United States flag planted upon the soil of Japan. A captain in the Union Army occupied the house for a time after he left it, and this flag was kept flying every day before the front door.

There is an interesting old graveyard about a mile from the town, which contains a number of very old graves, and soldiers of three wars are buried there. The first duel ever fought in the vicinity of Bladensburg was fought in this old graveyard.

The water of the famous spring near the turnpike is cool and delicious, and possesses great medicinal properties.

During the late war, when the country around the town was one great military camp, the soldiers, always on the lookout for good water, having once tasted of this spring, would not be satisfied with any other. It is said they would come several miles for it, bringing large barrels and wagons in which to carry it back to camp.

The notoriety given to Bladensburg by the duels fought near it, is the least interesting feature of the place. Too many valuable lives have been sacrificed, too many loving hearts made to ache in consequence of an erroneous interpretation of "the code," for one to derive any pleasure from dwelling upon the history of them. It is a satisfaction to know that more than thirty years have passed since there was a so-called "affair of honor" in its neighborhood.

XXVIII

MOUNT VERNON.

IN 1759 the Reverend Andrew Burnaby visited Mount Vernon, and wrote the following description of it: "This place is the property of Colonel Washington, and truly deserving of its owner. The house is most beautifully situated upon a very high hill on the banks of the Potomac, and commands a noble prospect of water, of cliffs, of woods, and plantations. The river is near two miles broad, though two hundred from the mouth; and divides the dominions of Virginia from Maryland."

One hundred and twenty-three years have passed away since that visit, and the mansion still stands upon a high hill, "and commands a noble prospect of water, of cliffs, and of woods," and is to-day undoubtedly the most interesting spot in the United States of America.

It is reached by boat from Washington, and from

the moment of leaving the wharf in the morning, until the hour the boat returns in the afternoon, the trip is one of peculiar pleasure. The scenes and incidents of three wars have made the country along the shore upon either side of the river deeply interesting, and the very name of the river rarely fails to send a thrill through the heart of those who, twenty years ago, had loved ones encamped along its banks awaiting the order to go forward to battle.

The distance is only sixteen miles, but the sail occupies about one hour and a half, as there are several stopping places before reaching the landing.

The approach to the landing is made known by the tolling of the bell—a courtesy never omitted by any boat upon the river—and the Superintendent stands ready at the wharf to receive and to entertain visitors. He leads the way to the tomb and mansion, and points out and explains all objects of interest.

The estate originally comprised several thousand acres, but at the present time there are only two hundred attached to the mansion; this was purchased in 1858 by the women of America, and in 1860 the association was incorporated under the title of "Ladies' Mount Vernon Association." The

place was very much out of repair when they purchased it, and Congress voted them a few thousand
dollars to make the repairs necessary for its preservation. The ladies struggled manfully to free it from
debt, but up to the beginning of the Centennial year
had not succeeded in doing so. The many thousands
of tourists, of that eventful year, who visited Philadelphia, extended their trip to the Capital, or at least
a large proportion did, and before the close of the
year Mount Vernon was free from debt. One dollar
is charged for the round trip, one-half of which goes
to the Association and the other half to the boat.

The mansion, that is the central part, was built by
Lawrence Washington, a half brother of General
Washington, and named in honor of Admiral Vernon, under whom he had served in the West Indies.
Lawrence was older than George and suffered for a
long time from ill health. His brother was his constant companion and attendant, and devoted much
time to him, and in return for this care Lawrence
left him the estate.

After Colonel Washington married the beautiful
and charming Mrs. Custis, he added wings to the
mansion and erected stables, smoke-house, kitchen,
and laundry. He also improved the grounds, and

laid out a large garden in beds and walks, and bordered them with neat box-wood hedges after the fashion of the time.

The mansion, although constructed of wood, is quite imposing and the situation one of great beauty. There is a wide hall-way and several spacious rooms upon the first floor. In the hall, secured in a small glass case against the wall, is the iron key of the famous Bastile, presented to Washington by Lafayette. It remains precisely where it was first placed by the illustrious recipient.

The rooms of the first floor are the dining-room, library, east and west parlors, and State dining-room.

Nearly all contain interesting relics and articles of furniture once used by the family, which have been gathered piece by piece at different times.

The furniture, camp-equipage, arms, and pictures are particularly interesting; but I must confess I never had any fancy for looking at old clothes and other articles once worn by distinguished persons. Locks of hair, half-worn slippers, bits of jewelry, and such things should be reserved for the sight of those to whom the wearer was bound by ties of affection and blood, and not be laid open to the gaze of the curious multitude.

20

Rembrandt Peale's picture of Washington before Yorktown is in the State dining-room, also a model of the Bastile, made from a piece of the fortress, a chair brought over in the "Mayflower," and many other things. The Superintendent says that more than 30,000 persons have sat down in this chair.

The mantel of this room is of fine white marble carved in Italy. The vessel conveying it to this country was seized upon the high seas by a French ship-of-war and the cargo taken possession of; but as soon as the commanding officer learned this mantel belonged to Washington he immediately returned it to him.

Upon the second floor the rooms are quite small, and hardly in keeping with the spacious dimensions of those of the first.

The room Lafayette occupied when a guest at Mount Vernon still contains the dressing-table and glass used by him when he made his last visit.

The room in which Washington died is very small, and has but one window. The bedstead is the very same upon which he breathed his last. It was returned by Mrs. Lee a year or two ago.

Still higher up is the small attic room to which Lady Washington retired after the death of her husband, and which she rarely ever left during the remainder of her life. It is apparently the worst in the house, and was selected because she could see from the window the tomb of him who was dearer to her than life, and she spent much of her time in gazing out upon it. In the door of the room is a small hole—cut to allow a favorite cat to pass in and out.

Mrs. Washington was a model wife and a famous housekeeper, and did not disdain to enter her kitchen and prepare with her own hands dainty dishes of all kinds. Her wines, cordials, and jellies were celebrated in the neighborhood, and one of her pleasures was to send such things around as gifts to her sick friends and neighbors. The roomy old kitchen, with its immense fireplace, is still standing, and one delights to go back in fancy and picture the scenes of that time when the dignified mistress graced it with her presence and directed the servants in preparing those tempting dinners and charming suppers for which the mansion was so famous. One of the prettiest word pictures we have of this notable housewife in her own home, was drawn by a guest after partaking of her hospitality one evening. He says: "The table of dark mahogany, waxed and polished like a mirror, was square. In the centre stood a branched *epergne* of silver wire and cut glass, filled with a tasteful arrangement of apples, pears, plums, peaches, and grapes. At one end Mrs. Washington, looking as handsome as ever, assisted by a young lady, presided behind a handsome silver tea-service. There was an enormous silver hot-water urn nearly two feet high, and a whole battalion of tiny flaring cups and saucers of blue India china. The silver, polished to its highest, reflected the blaze of many wax candles in branched candelabras and in sticks of silver. Fried oysters, waffles, fried chicken, cold turkey, canvas-backed ducks, venison, and that Southern institution, a 'baked ham,' were among the good things provided for the company of gentlemen invited by the President to sup with him. Lady Washington dispensed the tea with so much grace that each gentleman was constrained to take it, although capital Madeira was served in elegant decanters."

The master of the house was a successful farmer, and as much interested in his experiments as his wife was in her department. He took great pride in his estate, and devoted much time to improving and beautifying it. I believe there are several trees now standing planted by his own hand.

Across the river front of the mansion is a high, old-fashioned porch supported by square, wooden pillars. The floor of this porch is paved with large stone flags brought originally from the Isle of Wight. They are here and there worn into deep ridges by the tread of many feet, for every day brings some one to this interesting spot.

Republican and Democrat, citizen and soldier, tourists from foreign lands, members of the Diplomatic Corps, all come to this Mecca of America, where the gentle breezes from Virginia's hills make soft music in the branches of the pines and oaks, where the calm, silvery Potomac flows lazily around the grassy slopes, giving beauty and life to the quiet scene.

One feels inclined to moralize while standing beside the tomb, yet, after all, the occupants sleeping there so quietly are much better off than are many of the living. They have fought the battle of life, and have fought it successfully ; whereas, in a country like ours, of such rapid changes and fleeting honors, their fate might have been very different if the magician's wand could have imparted to them perpetual youth. Instead of being honored and revered, as their memory is to-day by all men, they might have become subjects of intrigue, indifference, and, possibly, scorn.

During the late war the tomb was neutral ground, and it is said soldiers of both armies would leave their arms miles away and meet there as brothers. Only one act of desecration occurred during the time the war lasted, and was committed by a thoughtless soldier, who climbed in over the iron gate, cut off and carried away one claw of the marble eagle upon the mausoleum of Washington. It was not known at the time who committed the deed, but he afterwards boasted of it in New York, and thereby incurred more reproach than congratulations for performing such a feat.

There was a story current for some time that the key to the gate of the tomb had been thrown into the river, so that it would be impossible for any one ever to open it again.

Upon inquiry, I learned this was only a pretty legend prepared for the benefit of the credulous.

INDEX.

A.

21

www.ingramcontent.com/pod-product-compliance
Lightning Source LLC
Chambersburg PA
CBHW020322140726
47905CB00013B/2152